D1179726

TISH
MARCHES ON

Books by
MARY ROBERTS RINEHART

Autobiography
MY STORY

Novels
THE DOCTOR
THIS STRANGE ADVENTURE
LOST ECSTASY
THE AMAZING INTERLUDE
K
A POOR WISE MAN
DANGEROUS DAYS
THE STREET OF SEVEN STARS
LONG LIVE THE KING
THE BREAKING POINT
THE STATE VERSUS ELINOR NORTON
TWO FLIGHTS UP
WHEN A MAN MARRIES
WHERE THERE'S A WILL

Mysteries
THE DOOR
THE AFTER HOUSE
THE ALBUM
THE CIRCULAR STAIRCASE
THE CASE OF JENNIE BRICE
THE MAN IN LOWER TEN
THE RED LAMP
SIGHT UNSEEN and THE CONFESSION
MISS PINKERTON
THE WINDOW AT THE WHITE CAT

Short Stories
AFFINITIES AND OTHER STORIES
BAB: A SUB-DEB
LOVE STORIES
MARRIED PEOPLE
MR. COHEN TAKES A WALK
TEMPERAMENTAL PEOPLE
THE ROMANTICS
THE TRUCE OF GOD
TWENTY-THREE AND A HALF HOURS' LEAVE
THE AMAZING ADVENTURES OF LETITIA CARBERRY
TISH
MORE TISH
TISH PLAYS THE GAME
TISH MARCHES ON

Travel
NOMAD'S LAND
TENTING TONIGHT
THE OUT TRAIL
THROUGH GLACIER PARK

War
KINGS, QUEENS AND PAWNS
THE ALTAR OF FREEDOM

Tish Marches On

By

Mary Roberts Rinehart

FARRAR & RINEHART, INC.

NEW YORK   TORONTO

COPYRIGHT, 1929, 1930, 1936, 1937, BY MARY ROBERTS RINEHART
PRINTED IN THE UNITED STATES OF AMERICA
BY THE FERRIS PRINTING COMPANY, NEW YORK
ALL RIGHTS RESERVED

CONTENTS

STRANGE JOURNEY

STRANGE JOURNEY

I

RECENTLY I have been pasting up the album in which for some years I have kept the record of such of Letitia Carberry's achievements as have reached the public press. Among them, in a separate box and marked "Snark," I find three small pieces of paper as well as a number of newspaper cuttings, and it occurs to me that the two are closely related. Also that the general public, bewildered at the time by certain published articles, has never been told the facts behind such headlines as "Man Partly Nude On Church Steeple. Fire Engines To Rescue"; or that one in the London *Times* on page fourteen, where it hides most of the news, entitled: "Unusual Discovery On A Sussex Golf Course."

There is also no adequate explanation given for the picture of the constable with the bandage around his head, the line beneath merely saying: "Victim Of Attack From Air." As for the other one, showing Aggie's red flannel petticoat with the bullet hole through it, she has never seen it, and I hope she never will.

Nevertheless, these clippings in a way do form a record of that strange experience of ours last spring. Some of them have a degree of accuracy. Thus I find a small clipping from a local New Jersey paper which

3

relates that a fisherman, going out one morning to his nets, had reported seeing a small dirigible balloon not far above the surface of the water and moving at what he estimated was one hundred miles an hour. And not only that. As he watched it he had seen it blown up and disappear. Being headed "A New Fisherman's Story" it probably attracted no attention, but it had a basis in fact.

On the other hand, there is no truth whatever in the one entitled: "Local resident shot in leg. Balloon bandits attack grocer." That was purely accidental, as I shall show, and we never even saw the man.

The three small pieces of paper already referred to are merely the clues from the Ostermaiers' hunt dinner, a charity party given each year for the Poor Fund, and at which one hunts his food by means of small verses of poetry. As Mr. Ostermaier is our clergyman, we always attend such functions, and I have included these clues since they form the real starting point of our adventure.

Or am I right? Did it not really begin earlier, when Charlie Sands, Tish's nephew, was preparing to report the Coronation in England for his paper and Tish expressed a desire to go with him?

Usually the most amiable of men, he refused this firmly.

"You're not going," he said. "I know you, and—well, you're not going."

"Don't be ridiculous," said Tish. "What harm could I do?"

"That," he said solemnly, "only you and your Creator can figure out. All I say is that these people

want to crown a king, and that they have their hands
full already."

"That is idiotic," said Tish irritably. "All I ask is
to get inside the Abbey and—"

"Yeah?" he said. "And have me wake from a
sweet dream of peace to see the Archbishop of Can-
terbury putting the crown on you! You're going to
stay home, and that's flat."

I have seldom seen him so firm, and at last Tish
reluctantly abandoned the project. He sailed soon
after on the *Crostic,* and we saw him off, giving him
a bottle of blackberry cordial as a remedy against
seasickness; but he did not seem really easy until
the ship moved out and he could look over the railing
and observe us safe on the pier below.

How well I remember his last words, shouted from
a distance but still clearly audible:

"Now remember," he called. "Don't try to pull
anything or I'll—"

We did not hear the rest, but as people were looking at us strangely we at once left the dock.

Yes, I believe that the adventure began that day.
Not that Tish bore any resentment, but that she had
a very real sense of frustration. She was silent as we
left New York and motored home again, speaking
only once.

"I dare say the time has come," she said, "when
I must settle down to my knitting and let the world
go by."

"Well, thak goodess for that," said Aggie, who
had her usual spring cold.

But I myself regard the words as more or less

prophetic. The time was indeed coming when all any
of us could do was to knit and let the world go by.

It was the next evening that the Ostermaiers gave
their hunt dinner, which as I have explained is one
where the guests, given various clues, are then obliged
to search for their food. I have three of these clues
before me as I write, and they look innocent in the
extreme. Who could believe that they would lead to
that awful moment when, helpless as we were, we
were obliged to leave our poor Aggie in her terrible
predicament? Or that discovering an entirely
strange young man searching for soup under the
Ostermaiers' guest-room bed would ultimately send
us whirling to the far places of the world?

No one, I am certain. . . .

I have reread all this material with varying emo-
tions. The *Snark* moves through it, a pale gray ghost
ultimately to die in a foreign land, and to be found
to contain two fish, still alive. But through it all also
moves Letitia Carberry, brave and indomitable.
Even at the worst she never lost courage, and she
should be, I think, an example to us all.

She was, I recall, strangely reluctant to go to the
dinner; but as it is given for charity, we all three
finally decided to attend. On the way there she commented on the staleness of life, and her extreme dislike of searching in people's closets for food which
would not be fit to eat anyhow.

"I begin to feel my age, Lizzie," she said sadly.
"With life consisting only of taxes, and government a racket, I long for a desert island and peace."

She was, however, somewhat more cheerful when

we reached the party, even showing some of her old enthusiasm when she received the first clue. It read:

> *At certain times its feet are four*
> *But sometimes they are six or more*
> *The burglar's joy, the spinster's fear*
> *You'll find your jellied soup is here.*

Tish gave it one glance and started up the stairs. "Too simple," she said. "Probably the whole parish is up there."

But when she led us into the Ostermaiers' guest room it was apparently empty. Only apparently, for in a moment we saw a pair of feet projecting from under the bed, and a second later a strange young man with his hair in a dreadful state sat up with a cup of cold soup in his hand and glared at us.

"Who the hell had *this* idea?" he demanded.

"You came to a hunt dinner, didn't you?" Tish inquired, with her usual dignity.

He looked at her queerly.

"But I thought—well, no matter what I thought," he added hastily. "Anyhow, here we are. Now what do we do?"

"You get first prize on soup."

He seemed slightly dazed.

"I see," he said. "First prize on soup. I've got a prize or two in my life, but never on soup. What do I get? A medal?"

"You can get some soup for us, if you don't mind," Tish observed, rather tartly.

He colored at that, said "Sorry!" and dived under

the bed again. When he emerged he had torn his coat on a broken bedspring, but he was more cheerful.

"I begin to get the hang of it," he said. "Do we eat this now, or go after the next prize? You see, I'm a stranger here."

Well, he seemed rather a pleasant person. There was nothing, then or later, to warn us that he was to be our Nemesis; or that the last time we were to see him, some days later, he would be giving us a look of plain, unadulterated hatred. His name he said was Blane, Jefferson Blane, although mostly called Jeff, and that he was motoring through with a girl; but that as soon as they arrived at the house she had paired off with another man.

"That's my usual luck," he said. "I bring 'em. They take 'em. Well, what about the second course?"

We got the clue, and it read:

Be quick. The night air's cold and chill,
This runs both ways but yet stands still,
Beneath it, humble, is the dish
Which you will find contains your fish."

It was puzzling. Tish said the only thing she knew of that ran both ways but remained in the same place was Aggie's nose, she being given to attacks of hay fever. Mr. Blane said it was the stairs, which certainly ran both ways; but a search of the closet beneath them only producing some old rubbers, we at last went out to the kitchen steps, and he found the fish in a new garbage can under them.

"It gets into the blood, doesn't it?" he said, mopping his face. "Do I get first prize for the garbage can also?"

Here, however, he saw a very pretty girl with a tall blond youth, and breathed heavily.

"If I was as good at women as I am at food," he said despondently, "I would take that girl out and wallop her within an inch of her life. Well, forget it. What's next?"

The next clue, however, eluded him.

> *Above the ground, unlike the rabbit,*
> *This creature rests, as is its habit.*
> *A case of nerves will show the wise*
> *To where it lays no more, but lies.*

"Child's play," he said cheerfully. "Hens, hence chickens. No pun intended. But what's a case of nerves? Hysterics? Hip something. I've got it— hypochondria! By Jove, do you suppose that stout woman over there is sitting on it?"

It was Aggie who, having suffered from them, remembered shingles, and I then suggested the porch roof. This was correct, but it is a part of the inevitability of our catastrophe that a blond girl and a man were already on the way there, and that Mr. Blane shoved past them almost rudely.

"Sorry," he said. "But *this* chicken is going to be mine."

"Why, Jeff Blane!" said the girl. "How dare you?"

I dare say it was due to this haste that Mr. Blane slipped as he stepped out onto the roof, and the next thing we heard was a rending of cloth followed by a thump below. The girl screamed.

"Jeff!" she called anxiously. "Are you hurt?"

"What do you care?" he said with some bitterness.

She spoke again, but he did not reply; and it was some time later that, taking an early departure, we perceived a figure lurking in the bushes and saw it edging furtively toward us.

It was Mr. Blane.

"Listen," he said. "If you care to inspect that porch roof back there you will find a largish piece of cloth. And if you care to inquire—not investigate—it's the seat out of my trousers. I thought," he added plaintively, "that you might have some suggestions."

How simple, yet how inevitable! What was more obvious than that Tish with her customary kindness should take him to her apartment and there present him with a pair of trousers belonging to Charlie Sands? Yet before he left he had sowed the wind and we were to reap the whirlwind. I think he should remember this. Certainly to say, as he has said, that we deliberately left him on that church steeple a few days later is not only entirely false. It is most ungrateful.

II

It was after he was clothed and had had a glass or two of our blackberry cordial that the fatal incident occurred. He had, I remember, stated that he was a visitor to our city, and that he was not strong enough for our type of hunt dinners. Also that blondes were fickle and that he was entirely washed up—whatever that meant.

But it was when he walked over and inspected a large mounted tarpon which Tish had captured some years before that he really planted the seed of trouble.

"Where I come from," he said contemptuously, "we'd call that thing a minnow."

"What do you fish for?" Tish inquired coldly. "Whales?"

Well, it turned out that he fished for sharks, and that—of all things—from a small dirigible. He said that it was perfectly simple. You merely cruised until you saw a large one, and then dropped the hook and bait more or less in its mouth.

"Greatest sport in the world," he said. "Shoot them through the head, of course, before you pull them in."

Tish was so interested that Aggie gave me a look of pure agony and sneezed violently.

"Get hib away, Lizzie," she implored me. "Look at her!"

Certainly Tish was intensely interested. She had put down her knitting and was gazing at him thoughtfully.

"What bait do you use?" she inquired.

"A dead horse is good. White, if you can find one. But pork will do. They like pork."

He talked about it for some time and poor Aggie was quite pale when, after a final glass of cordial, he prepared to depart—in Charlie Sands' trousers.

"If you ever want to try it," he said, "just call up Johnnie Smith at Green Harbor. He'll fix you so you can go and have yourselves a time."

Yes, that was what he said. And my reply is that we did, and that we had!

I did not like the look in Tish's face after Mr. Blane had gone; and to make matters worse, Aggie had a return of her jaundice that night and itched violently until morning.

Nevertheless, for a day or so all was quiet. Tish received a radiogram from Charlie Sands in that interval: "On no account alter decision," which she resented somewhat; and both Aggie and I noticed that she had an absent look in her eyes. Also she complained of lumbago. But we were not suspicious until one evening Hannah, her maid, came to see us and reported a strange condition of affairs.

"I don't believe it, Hannah," I said severely.

"You ask the janitor," Hannah said tearfully. "She dropped one, and some of it fell on his head. It cost her twenty dollars to square him. And as for that policeman—"

"What policeman?"

"He put his motorcycle down below and the hook caught it. When he saw it crawling up the wall he yelled like anything. Then the line broke, and it as near as anything killed him, Miss Lizzie."

(I may interpolate here that this was an overstatement. The man was merely bruised. As for the city claiming damages for the motorcycle, that is ridiculous. Why do we pay taxes?)

It was some time before we got the entire story.

Apparently Tish had been practicing hauling heavy weights up to her apartment, doing so at night when the courtyard was empty. For this purpose she had employed a pail filled with coal, fishing for the handle with a large hook on a line. Then—the night before—the motorcycle incident had occurred, and we gathered from Hannah that she had given up the idea.

"And what is she doing tonight, Hannah?" I inquired.

Hannah sniffled.

"That's what I came about," she said. "She's cleaning her rifle. That means trouble, Miss Lizzie. I know her."

We sent Hannah home after that, but we both spent a wretched evening. With Charlie Sands on the high seas we felt completely helpless, and when the next morning Tish sent for us we knew that protest would be useless.

We found her surprisingly cheerful, and the entire place seemed to be littered with fishing lines, ropes, chains, and enormous hooks. She put down a large hook when we entered.

"Lizzie," she said abruptly. "What do you know about sharks?"

It had come! But I pretended to ignore it.

"What sort of sharks?" I said. "Bridge sharks? Loan sharks? Or stock market sharks?"

"Don't be a fool," she observed. "Ordinary sharks."

"Only that they have teeth. Too many teeth."

"Do you know that their skins are valuable?"

"So is mine, Tish," I said tartly. "And I don't intend to risk it. I go in no dirigible, and I dangle no piece of pork before a shark's nose. As far as I am concerned, there are no sharks."

I am glad that I made that protest, useless as it proved to be. For things had gone further than I had anticipated. Not only had she written to Mr. Smith. She had already engaged the *Snark*—which was the blimp: shall I ever forget it?—for the next day.

She eyed us both sternly.

"You have your choice," she said. "Either you come or I go alone."

What could we do? Never before had we deserted her, and so at last we agreed. But Aggie was in such an acute state of terror that evening that during the night I heard a crash and found that she had fallen out of bed. When I found her she was on the floor, apparently trying to swim in the water from an upset pitcher.

"Help!" she said, in a smothered voice. "Help! I'm drowdig!"

It was some time before I could convince her that she was still safe in her room, and not in the Atlantic Ocean.

Fortunately we were kept busy the next day. There was not only the matter of food to arrange. Tish had reminded us that the upper levels of the air were cool, which explains Aggie's red flannel petticoat later. We also purchased a small alcohol stove and a kettle for tea, a frying pan, and packed a substantial amount of food, including a quantity of eggs. This, with bottled water, some blackberry cordial, and Tish's rifle, completed our equipment; and we left late in the afternoon by car for Green Harbor.

The last thing we did was to purchase our bait, forty pounds of pork cut into two pound pieces, and Mr. Beilstein looked rather surprised.

"That's a lot of pork, Miss Carberry," he said. "What are you going to do? Start a barbecue stand?"

"We are going fishing," said Tish with her usual dignity, and he was still on the pavement staring after us as we drove away.

Tish was her optimistic self during the journey. She had already calculated that she could increase her income considerably, and that fish caught beyond the three-mile limit should not be taxable.

"It may be," she said, "that we have at last found a method of legal evasion which the Congress has not discovered. And there are millions of sharks in the sea."

Aggie, however, refused to be comforted.

"Thed let theb stay there," she said hollowly. "*I dod't wadt ady.*"

Yet, looking back, I realize that Aggie was in better condition than I had expected. She was sneezing less, for one thing, and at the hotel that night she ate quite a good dinner. I know the reason now, and can understand her perfidy. Yet, in view of the fact that she had already sent that warning radiogram to Charlie Sands, I can only feel that she deserved some of her later misfortunes. To blame Letitia Carberry, as she has, is most unfair.

We were up quite early, and after a breakfast of scrambled eggs—which Aggie ate over my protest—we drove to the flying field. Mr. Smith was there, and so was the dirigible which he called the *Snark*. It was already out in the open with the engines·going, and a dozen men or so were holding it down by what he called the handling lines, or ropes. Mr. Smith seemed very proud of it.

"Pretty, isn't she?" he said. "And willing! She'd go on forever if you'd let her."

Willing! As I write that word my hand fairly trembles. If ever a dirigible was willing it was that one.

Tish was the first to get into the thing, and while the lunch et cetera was being carried aboard he explained to her how the dirigible was operated. It had a wheel to the right of the pilot seat, to raise and lower it, and two foot pedals to steer by. Also it had two engines, he said, and when fishing for sharks one of them had to be stopped or the line would be caught.

"Well, that's the ship," he said. "Safe and comfortable. You'll never forget this experience, ladies. And the boys say there's a lot of sharks offshore. . . . Hello!" he said suddenly. "What's all this?"

I looked, and a girl was driving up in a small car. She got out in a hurry and rushed toward us.

"Johnnie!" she called.

I knew her at once. It was the blond girl at the Ostermaiers', and she had been crying.

"What's wrong?" Mr. Smith inquired.

"Listen, Johnnie. It's Jeff. He's lost. You'll have to find him."

"You couldn't lose Jeff Blane anywhere in the Atlantic," said Mr. Smith.

"He wants to be lost," said the girl desperately. "We had a quarrel yesterday and he started out to sea in his boat. He said he'd go straight out until the gas ran out. And he hasn't come back. You know him, Johnnie," she added. "He's stubborn. He'll do it."

"Yeah," said Mr. Smith thoughtfully. "Jeff's stubborn, all right. He might do it."

"You could throw him a rope and tow him back, couldn't you?" And here she said something which I find hard to forgive, and which was responsible for much of our later trouble. "Hurry, Johnnie," she said. "Get those awful old women out and hurry."

I saw Tish stiffen. But at that moment a messenger boy rode up on a bicycle, and Aggie looked cheerful for the first time that morning.

"Got a radiogram for Mr. Smith," said the boy. "Where is he?"

"Here," said Mr. Smith.

"Got to come down and sign for it."

I believe that Tish even then had an inkling of the truth. Mr. Smith went down the ladder, signed the slip and read the message. Then he took off his cap and, scratching his head, walked over slowly and shouted up to Tish.

"I've got a message here, Miss Carberry. Seems like somebody named Sands says you're not to go. Says he's your nephew. Says he absolutely forbids

it. Seems like a pity, doesn't it? Good day and everything."

"Nonsense," said Tish sharply. "I am of legal
age."

He scratched his head again.

"Still and all," he said, "we like the consent of the
family. If your nephew doesn't like the idea—"

"Does that mean you refuse to take us?"

"I guess it does."

I should have known what would happen. I have
known Tish Carberry for many years. I know her
courage and her strength of will. But who could
have guessed that she would turn away from that
window, grab the wheel, press a number of things at
random, and suddenly shoot that wretched contraption up into the air as if it had been fired out of a
gun? . . .

When I picked myself up I saw the men on the field
below laid out flat like a row of ninepins. We shaved
the top of a barn, and a moment later I had the
anguish of seeing one of our dangling ropes whip
around a clothesline and jerk an entire family washing high in the air. There was a woman beside it with
her arms up, ready to hang a garment on it; and she
simply remained in that position, as if it could not
have occurred.

How can I express my sensations at that time,
alone as we were in the air and moving rapidly in
various directions as Tish experimented with the
mechanism? Or my horror when, on looking for
Aggie, I could not see her at all? But at that moment
a faint sneeze reassured me, and I found her wedged

under the rear seats of the cabin, with the basket of eggs on her chest and her eyes closed.

"Aggie!" I cried in terror.

She did not open her eyes.

"By chest is crushed, Lizzie,"she said sadly. "I caddot breathe. Let be die id peace."

I removed the basket, but she still remained as she was.

"Why should I get up?" she demanded. "I have years ad years to get up id."

"What on earth do you mean?"

"How are we goig to get dowd?" she inquired, still with her eyes shut.

"We seem to be going down this minute," I retorted with some irritation.

This, however, was a mistake. Tish was merely experimenting with the controls, and as a result the chip was behaving like a bucking horse, rising, dropping, and then shooting ahead iu a most terrifying manner.

She was her usual calm self, though.

"I see now how it works," she said. "It is entirely simple."

As Aggie chose this moment to be violently airsick, I made no reply. Holding our poor companion as she leaned out of a window, I was able to see that Tish had at least been able to bring up the ropes. But also I discovered that she was not turning back. That she was indeed headed directly toward the open sea. As soon as possible, therefore, I went to her and entered a protest.

"I am in no mood, Tish," I said, "to fish for sharks. I insist that you turn around and go back."

"And leave Mr. Blane to die?" she inquired. "You surprise me, Lizzie. When have I ever evaded a plain duty, especially where youth and its problems are involved?"

Unfortunately Aggie had heard her, and went even paler.

"Mr. Blade!" she said. "Ad what will we do with hib whed we get hib?"

I must confess that the same thought was in my mind, but Tish remaining silent and the *Snark* now on even keel, I had only my own thoughts for company.

It was not long before we passed over the beach and were at last above the sea. With what anguish I watched the shores recede! With what torture of mind did I see far beneath us a gray line of battleships, our protection in time of war but of no use to us at that time. With what envy did I see here and there a fishing boat, busy with its peaceful occupation of capturing the finny creatures of the deep.

Feeling as I did, I was shocked an hour or so later to have Tish request me to prepare the shark tackle.

"Really, Tish," I protested.

But I had no time for more. She was pointing far ahead.

"Unless I am wrong," she said, "that is Mr. Blane. We must prepare to save him."

Well, there was a small boat there, and through the glasses we could see it had an occupant, a man bare above the waist and wearing only bathing trunks. I have since read Mr. Blane's statement, that he had plenty of gas and was quietly fishing when—as he calls it—he was attacked. This may be true, but there can be no doubt that he stood up when he saw the *Snark* and waved to it. If we were mistaken in regarding this as a signal of distress, I am sorry. He suffered, I admit; but we suffered more. Much, much more.

However that may be, Tish at once instructed me to prepare the shark tackle and, after securing one end of the line to the structure of the dirigible, to lower it from the open door to the surface of the water.

"I shall slacken speed," she said, "and it will then be your duty to engage the hook in the bow of the boat. In this manner we can tow him back to land, and all will be well."

I still maintain that this plan, however it worked out, was both feasible and well intended, as are all of Letitia Carberry's. Indeed, as we approached and our speed slackened, he looked up at us with quite a pleasant smile and waved again.

"Hello!" he called. "Seen any sharks yet?"

But all at once his expression changed, and too late I saw what was happening. A slight puff of wind hit us at the moment, and the shark hook was moving directly toward him and was about to strike him. He ducked hastily to avoid it, and then occurred the dreadful thing which still haunts my dreams.

The hook caught him by the belt of his bathing trunks and lifted him bodily out of the boat.

III

Never shall I forget that moment, with Mr. Blane dangling face down far beneath us, and Aggie wailing feebly that she wanted to go home.

Nor was this all. The worst was still to come. For not only was he a heavy man, but on attempting to lift him the chain above the hook caught on the ladder, which was still over the side, and do what we could we were unable to liberate it. It was therefore with a sober face that Tish at last turned the *Snark* toward the land again.

"We must find assistance," she observed. "By going close to the ground he may be able to catch hold of something and thus free himself. Or the men at the landing field can catch him. There is no reason for despair."

"Not udless his belt breaks," said Aggie darkly.

I have explained this in detail to show our real solicitude at the time. We did not kidnap Mr. Blane. We did not attack him. That the chain caught as it did was purely accidental. Indeed, we went so far as to lower a bottle of blackberry cordial on a line, to relieve somewhat the anxiety of his position, and he reached for it eagerly. In his constrained position, however, the attempt to swallow brought on a severe attack of coughing, and we were terrified lest his slender support give way.

I need not say how grateful we were when at last the shores of our beloved country came in sight. I remember that even Aggie rallied from her lethargy of despair.

"By dear, by dative lad!" she said. "Ad if ever I set foot od it agaid I'll dever leave it."

Poor Aggie! When I think what even then was before her my very spirit quails.

Nevertheless, when we reached the land another blow was in store for us. It was completely unfamiliar, and there was no sign whatever of the flying field. Moreover, although we saw plenty of people, none of them seemed surprised at our strange burden, or made any effort to help. Indeed, I have learned since that it was regarded as a movie stunt of some sort, and I believe there are still extant a number of photographs showing Mr. Blane in his strange situation.

Even Tish became seriously annoyed, the more so as no landing field of any sort was visible.

"The dratted idiots!" she said. "Look out for a haystack, Lizzie. We'll have to put him somewhere."

It was, I think, at that time that Aggie roused to make a remark which I was to remember later.

"I wish," she said viciously, "that Charlie Sads could see us dow."

I have seldom lived through a more anxious time. Now and then over the roar of the engines we could hear Mr. Blane's voice, and he seemed to be shouting. We could not hear what he said, however. Then at last Tish slowed up the motors and leaned over the side.

"Ahoy below!" she called. "I am going down. Catch hold of a fence or something."

We dipped at once, and a team of horses attached to a farm wagon shied violently and then ran away.

We then passed over a golf course, and a number of people waved but made no effort to help us. At last, however, Mr. Blane managed to catch hold of some fencing and the situation was apparently saved. But at that moment a small breeze caught us, and he rose rapidly, carrying part of the fence with him.

(I wish here to state that, while it is true that he later dropped it on a cow, it was purely accidental, nor was the cow injured. That is shown by the speed with which she ran, and also by the way she jumped a quite high barbed-wire fence.)

It was while we were watching the cow that I heard Aggie scream.

"Tish!" she yelled. "The church steeple. He'll hit it!"

It was too late. There was a jerk and the *Snark* leaped up and forward, throwing us all off our feet. But when we looked back Mr. Blane was safely on the top of the steeple, holding to a lightning rod with one hand while with the other, his belt having given way, he clutched at his bathing trunks.

As we passed over him he turned his face up to us, and I regret to say that it was contorted with fury.

It was at this time that there occurred the other incident which was to bring us such opprobrium later. Tish felt that help was still required, as the church was a remote one, and on a leaf from my pocket memorandum book she wrote as follows: "Mr. Jefferson Blane on church steeple at crossroads. Please call local fire department to rescue."

This, lacking anything else, she tied to a shell from her rifle; when over the next town, she caught the

attention of a number of people and then dropped it.
To our dismay it fell into a chimney instead, and was
followed very shortly by a muffled report and a puff
of smoke and soot. I continue with the clipping mentioned earlier and headed "Local Resident Shot In
Leg."

"Not satisfied with what they had already done,
the bandits then proceeded to shoot from the dirigible, one bullet striking Mr. Peter Jenks, the well-
known grocer, who was reading his newspaper in
front of the fire. Fortunately it lodged in his artificial
leg, but Mr. Jenks is still in retirement, due to shock."

As we never saw Mr. Peter Jenks, the unfairness
of this report is obvious.

We circled for some time near the church steeple,
and at last had the happiness of seeing people running in that direction. But it was then that Tish made
one of her rare mistakes. We could, I am confident,
have discovered the flying field in time and thus have
been hauled down to earth; but here her conscience
intervened.

"Due to no fault of our own," she said, "we have
left Mr. Blane's motorboat to drift without guid-
ance and inevitably be lost. We must locate it again,
and bring it back."

No protests availing, we again headed for the
broad Atlantic. Tish was in excellent spirits, rejoic-
ing at having reunited the two young lovers, and
certain that their quarrel was over. But as we passed
over the naval vessels once more she grew more
sober.

"How strange it is," she observed, "to be high in

this beautiful air, secure from danger; and yet to see beneath us the murderous instruments of warfare. Nature," she added, "is kind. It is only man who is cruel."

It is at such moments that Tish is at her best.

How true, as we were to discover later!

We moved on. Aggie was now calm, if despairing. Tish was watching for Mr. Blane's boat and—it being almost noon by that time—I prepared a luncheon. Due to various causes the soup had been spilled, and the caramel custard was spread largely over the basket. Indeed, strangely enough, all that remained intact was our eggs; and over Aggie's protests we were reduced to scrambled eggs and tea again.

Thus reinforced, we all felt better, and Tish fell to planning how to rescue the boat without damage.

"If we can use the shark hook to bring up a handling rope," she said thoughtfully, "we can then make a loop in the rope and drop it, preferably over the steering wheel. After that it will be a simple matter to tow it back."

After some difficulty this was arranged, and as we had by this time seen what was apparently the boat far ahead, all appeared well. We lowered the loop into the water and prepared for action.

It was then that we saw the shark. It was coming from the coast directly toward us, swimming under the surface and moving with amazing rapidity. I recall Tish and her expression as she gazed down at it.

"I had no idea," she said thoughtfully, "that they swam so fast."

Those were the last words I heard her speak for some time!

Considering the situation now, I understand what followed. At the time, however, I only knew that there was a terrific jerk, and that without warning the *Snark* was brought close to the surface of the water and shot forward with astounding speed. This is undoubtedly when the fisherman saw us; however that may be, the result was shocking. All of us were thrown to the rear of the cabin, and to make matters worse, an occasional wave washed in and almost smothered us.

Nor was that all. We were up to our waists in water when Tish, gazing ahead, saw that we were approaching a floating structure, shaped roughly like a boat, and hastily called to us to hold on to something. The next moment there came a shocking explosion. We were showered with pieces of wood, and the *Snark,* abruptly released, rose high in the air and whirled about in a most dizzy fashion.

It was Tish who recovered first and rose slowly to her feet.

"That was a torpedo, Lizzie," she said, in a strange voice.

"Indeed!" I replied coldly. "I thought it was a shark that had swallowed some dynamite."

But she ignored me.

"It is quite evident what has happened," she observed. "The navy is at practice and the thing caught in the loop of our rope. It is extremely fortunate," she added, "that it struck the target. Otherwise we might be far at sea by this time."

I had no time to consider what might have happened. What had occurred was plenty. The fact is that a hasty survey had showed me no sign whatever of Aggie, and it was some time before, on wading to the rear of the cabin, I discovered her in the small lavatory installed there. So violent had been the impact that she was wedged tightly against a sanitary fixture, with only her head above water. And I can still see her gazing up at me with agonized eyes.

"I have lost by teeth, Lizzie," she said plaintively.

It was some time before we recovered them, luckily undamaged, and I regret to say that Aggie was in a most unpleasant humor. Not only had a small fish taken refuge about her person, but she had swallowed considerable sea water. She said with some bitterness that she had been a number of things in her time, but never an aquarium.

"Ad I'b full of water," she added indignantly. "Put a couple of hoops od be, ad I'd bake a good barrel."

However, I soon forgot her troubles. On emerging into the cabin I realized that something was seriously wrong. Tish was standing in the water, gazing ahead, and her face was sober as she turned to me.

"The engines have stopped, Lizzie," she said.

It was but too true.

Words fail me when I attempt to describe our situation. There was no land in sight. The cabin was awash, and no efforts of ours sufficed to open the door so that the water might escape. And our attemps at bailing—with the teakettle and frying pan —had little or no effect; indeed, they only revealed the variety of sea life we had picked up, including several fish, an eel or two, and a number of small crabs. (We evidently overlooked some fish, as the *Daily Mail* later stated that two were found in the *Snark,* quite alive, and adding to the mystery.)

As we were all drenched to the skin, we were obliged to remove such garments as we could and hang them up to dry. This we did by stretching a line, and what was later alluded to as our red flag was merely Aggie's flannel petticoat which, hanging near a window, blew out at intervals.

In addition to all this, we were drifting helplessly, now high above the waves and then close to the surface; and to add to our discomfort a storm was undoubtedly blowing up. There were huge clouds to the west, and the sky was darkening. No efforts of Tish's would start the motors, and it was with a sad heart that I prepared the evening meal of scrambled eggs and tea.

It was late at night when the storm hit us. As everyone remembers the hurricane of that date, I need say little about it. At first the rain was so heavy that we were beaten down until we could hear the wild waves beneath us. After that came the wind. It blew away some of our clothing, and at times whirled us about until at last it was necessary to tie ourselves to our seats.

Incredible as it may sound, that situation lasted for two full days. And as it now looked as though years later the *Snark* might be discovered in some remote part of the world, I felt it my duty to keep a record of our strange journey through the air.

I reproduce here one day only, as the other was the same. It follows:

"Monday, 8 A.M. Wind still blowing. Breakfast of scrambled eggs and tea.

"Monday, 12 Noon. Wind still blowing. Lunch of scrambled eggs and tea.

"Monday, 6 P.M. Wind still blowing. Supper of scrambled eggs and tea."

Tish's knitting had fortunately escaped the deluge, and she completed a pair of socks during this time. By constant bailing Aggie and I had somewhat reduced our water content; but it was a dreary interval, and Aggie's nerves began to suffer. The limited diet of eggs was not too good for her, and when on the second day we sighted an iceberg she at once demanded to be lowered to it.

"At least it is goig sobewhere," she said bitterly. "Ad I'd like to bet it dever heard of a scrabbled egg."

Dawn of the third day found us still in this painful situation, and fast in the clouds and fog. But that day the storm abated somewhat, and later on Tish glanced up from her knitting and gazed steadily ahead.

"I do not wish to encourage any false hopes," she said. "But there is a ship not far away. It is just possible that we are saved."

IV

What followed is almost certainly the origin of the published statement that a certain British liner was attacked at sea on that date by a Russian dirigible, flying the red flag; and the answer to the press reports, that the attack was evidently intended to cause an international situation and prevent the Coronation.

How preposterous! I can only state the facts, but they certainly speak for themselves.

In the first place, having sighted the ship, the fog closed in again and we almost immediately lost it. There was, however, a chance that we would pass near or even over it, and it was Tish's idea that in the latter case we anchor ourselves to it if possible. For this purpose we used all four of our landing ropes, fastening our largest hooks to them, and then dropping them over the side.

All of us then took up our positions at the windows, leaning out and watching with profound anxiety. What was our relief when we heard a foghorn close at hand, and suddenly saw the ship, in all its glory, directly beneath us There was a solitary man on the top deck, and we all saw him at the same time.

He saw us too, and never so long as I live shall I forget his face as he stared up at us. He seemed to stagger and then look again, and it did not require Aggie's frenzied sneezing to tell us who it was.

It was Charlie Sands!

The next instant one of our hooks caught firmly in the window of a small deckhouse beside him. He must have heard the sound, for he turned and looked at it. Then, to our horror, a blast of hot air from one of the funnels caught us and whirled us high in the air, and the structure was lifted bodily from the deck and collapsed with a loud crash.

Not only that. We had the agony of seeing a small piece of timber strike him, and of seeing him knocked from his feet!

There was of course nothing to be done. The *Snark* was moving on into the fog again, and the last we saw of Charlie Sands he was sitting upright amidst the wreckage, holding both hands to his head and gazing after us with a dazed look on his face.

This, I think, adequately explains the so-called attack on the *Crostic*. To state that we deliberately destroyed the wireless cabin and antennæ on that ship, thus leaving it temporarily helpless in fog and heavy seas, is entirely false; as is the statement referring to our red flag.

I must admit that the incident left us all rather shaken; especially what had happened to Charlie Sands. But after a luncheon of scrambled eggs and tea we felt stronger, and Tish was more her old and confident self.

"It is apparent," she observed, "that we have crossed the Atlantic and may soon be over foreign soil. In that case—"

"Id that case," said Aggie bitterly, "I suppose it will cobe up ad get us!"

For that was now our problem. Tish finished the second sock thoughtfully.

"We must be anchored to something," she observed. "We cannot run the risk of floating indefinitely over Europe, or of being blown back across the sea. It should be possible," she added, "for one of us to be lowered on a rope and thus make fast to some stationary object before it is too late."

Aggie at once burst into tears, but Tish's solution seemed to be the obvious one; the more so as—the fog now clearing—the *Snark* was seen to be not far above the surface of the water, and moving slowly before a gentle breeze. Not only was this the case. Not far ahead, and apparently anchored, was a small boatlike structure—shall I ever forget it?—which offered possibilities for the purpose.

"As the lightest of the three, Aggie," Tish remarked, "this duty should fall to you. I hope that you will do it cheerfully."

"What do you wadt be to do? Sig?" Aggie demanded.

In the end, however, she agreed; in a short time, the rope under her arms, we were lowering her carefully, and finally had the great joy of seeing her beneath us, safe and sound.

All would have been well, or at least better, had she been able at once to secure the rope. But unfortunately she had just then one of her violent sneezing attacks, the rope slipped out of her hands, and we had the agony of seeing it trailing in the water and leaving her behind.

It was too much. Leaning out a window we could see her anguished face, contorted for another sneeze, and the faint wave of her hand that was her feeble gesture of farewell.

Sad as this was, it was nothing to what followed. We had been puzzled by the fact that no crew had appeared on the boat, and we had drifted only a mile or so away when we understood. Tish caught my arm and pointed back to where our poor companion was now merely a small dot in the distance.

A plane was diving out of the clouds directly at her, and a moment later there was an explosion and a splash of water beside her.

It was then that we knew the truth. In a world threatened with war, an American torpedo had first left us helpless. Now foreign planes were using Aggie—and the boat—as a target!

How describe what followed? How explain our feelings as plane after plane dived from the sky, dropped its deadly charge, and rose again? What did it matter that, with the clearing of the weather, our gas expanded and we found ourselves high in the air again? Or that soon far beneath us we saw green fields and even a town or two? Our poor Aggie was lost, we feared, forever.

"And that is war," Tish said. "Attacking helpless women. Like little boys playing marbles, Lizzie! And to what end? To what end?"

I could make no reply.

I pass over the remainder of that day, which was endless. There was no gentle presence in the cabin, and Aggie's red petticoat waving in the wind was but a sad and tragic reminder. But our own situation was soon to become precarious. As evening fell and the gas contracted we began to descend, and darkness found us barely above the treetops.

Tish lowered our handling ropes again, in the hope that they would catch on something and anchor us. But soon matters took a serious turn. In passing over a small hamlet we brushed a number of chimneys, and could hear bricks falling and people shouting; and at last the unbelievable happened.

For some time we had heard small reports from below, and finally something struck the teakettle with a sharp ping.

Tish made a light and examined it.

"They are shooting at us, Lizzie," she said. "Throw out what you can. We must rise again."

This, I dare say, is the origin of the clipping entitled: "Constable Struck By Frying Pan," which lies before me now. But I must admit that the hostility shown to us, strangers as we were, puzzled us greatly. It was only later that we learned the facts: the steamer *Crostic,* having repaired its wireless, had warned that it had been attacked by a dirigible carrying a red flag, and that the entire country had been notified by the British Broadcasting Company to be on the alert.

But our strange journey was almost over. We had little to throw overboard. Soon we became aware of a hissing over our heads and realized that the branch of a tree or a chimney pot had torn the dirigible. Then we were bumping across a field, and at last were able to step onto terra firma again.

Never so long as I live shall I forget what followed. The *Snark,* wounded to death, lay behind us, a huddled and expiring mass; while along a number of roads motorcars, bicycles, and people afoot were converging on us.

The first to arrive was a constable on a motorcycle, with a bandage on his head and a most unpleasant manner. He at once caught Tish by the arm and held on to her.

"You'll come along with me," he said grimly. "Just about killed me, you did. We'll teach you Russians something you won't forget! Women, too! Aren't you ashamed of yourselves?"

"Russians!" said Tish. "Don't dare to call us that."

He seemed bewildered.

"Did you or did you not come in that dirigible?" he demanded.

Never have I so admired Tish as in this emergency. She drew herself up haughtily and stared at him.

"What dirigible?" she inquired coldly.

He let go of her arm, and as by that time a crowd was gathering, he turned fiercely on it.

" 'Op it," he said. " 'Op it and somebody ring the chief constable. I'll 'ave to stand by 'ere."

It was then that Tish turned to me and spoke in a low voice.

"We are in England, Lizzie," she said quietly.

It was indeed true. Driven by storm and wind, we had crossed the broad Atlantic and were now on a golf course in Sussex. But Tish's superb courage did not fail her, even then.

"We must get out of here as quickly as possible," she observed. "To be arrested would be indeed serious, as we have no passports. Also there is the possibility that Aggie has survived. In that case—"

She did not finish, but I understood; and I feel that the later statement that we stole a car that night and deliberately wrecked it is not justified. Our one thought was to proceed to London and notify the British Admiralty of Aggie's situation. As to wrecking the car, who would have believed that the English drive on the left side of the road?

As it happened, our escape was not difficult. The crowd was now dense and in the general excitement Tish led the way through it. Shortly after, we found ourselves in a lane, with what we have since learned was a fine Daimler car. The engine was running, and soon we had left the excitement behind us and were on a main road.

Driving proved exceedingly difficult, however, and even Tish was surprised.

"These people are crazy with excitement," she said. "Never again will I believe that they are stolid or phlegmatic. They are *all* on the wrong side."

Nevertheless, after some narrow escapes, we had put the remains of the *Snark* some ten miles or so behind us when trouble came. We struck a car head on, and I narrowly escaped going through the windshield. (This probably explains the statement that one of the escaping bandits was injured, as my nose bled quite badly.)

It was impossible to go on, especially as a man got out of the other car and began shouting at us.

"What the bloody h— do you mean, driving on the wrong side of the road?" he yelled. "You've broken my leg!"

"If you don't know your right hand from your left," Tish said, "why blame me?"

"A woman, by God!" he said profanely. "A woman, of course!"

He then started limping toward us, and once more flight became necessary. It was dawn and my nose had just stopped bleeding when at last we found a country inn and staggered inside. There was a woman there, and she regarded us with cold eyes.

"We would like a room, and something to eat," Tish said.

And I shall never forget my despair when she replied: "All I 'ave at this hour is some hot tea and maybe an egg or two."

We reached London and a small hotel later in the day, and in the interval while our clothing was being dried and pressed we sent out for all the newspapers. As I have said, the *Times* on page fourteen had a brief article entitled "Unusual Discovery On A Sussex Golf Course." But the *Daily Mail* had it spread all over the front page. There was a picture of the *Snark,* now merely a limp and huddled piece of canvas in a field. There was a picture of the constable with his bandage, entitled "Victim of Attack From Air." There was our poor Aggie's red petticoat, with a bullet hole through it, and beneath: "Was This Used As Red Flag?" And worst of all Tish's rifle was shown and captioned: "Are Armed Communists, Denied Passports, Reaching England By Air?"

Lacking clothing, we could not pursue our search for Aggie. It was necessary indeed to retire to our beds, and we had barely done so when there came a thunderous knocking at the door.

Almost immediately it opened, and there was Charlie Sands, with a policeman behind him and a most dreadful look on his face.

He gave us one glance and then turned to the officer.

"All right," he said briefly. "It's them. Stand by outside, will you?"

I fairly cringed when I had a good look at him. One eye was completely closed, and there was a large lump on his forehead. But he addressed himself to Tish.

"I presume," he said, "that you are the Communists. I gather that it was you who hit the constable with a frying pan. And I know damned well that you attacked the *Crostic*. Look at me and you'll know why. But what I want to know is if you did this."

He then jerked a newspaper from his pocket:

"A strange discovery was reported by the Royal Flying Corps today. At practice off the Solent they discovered a woman on a floating target.

"The woman was uninjured but suffering from shock and a slight attack of jaundice. She could tell no connected story, merely stating that she had reached the target by a rope, and that she and some friends were hunting sharks and that they had hung somebody on a church steeple.

"By her accent she is an American, but hospital authorities cannot be certain, as she had a heavy cold. Normal in some ways, she had an attack of shrieking hysteria when offered scrambled eggs and tea."

He read that aloud, and then stared at us malignantly through his one eye.

"I presume," he said, "that this is Aggie. What I want to know is, who did you hang on that church steeple? And why?"

It was then that Tish told him the story. Halfway through he sat down, as though his legs would not hold him. But he listened patiently.

"I see," he said at last. "Perfectly natural, all of it. I suppose it's that knock on the head that makes me dizzy. I gather," he added, "that you feel all right. You haven't a cold or anything?"

"Why should *I?*" Tish inquired.

He groaned and got up.

"That's it," he said in a strange voice. "You lasso a torpedo and it merely takes you for a ride. You put Aggie on a target and six good pilots fail to hit her. You hang a poor devil on a church steeple and even take the belt that holds up his trunks. You put a liner's wireless out of commission in a fog, practically destroy me, damage a Daimler car, and injure a peer of the realm—and you haven't even a sniffle. It is too much. Far, far too much. You ought to suffer. For two English farthings I would call in that officer and send you to jail."

Fortunately, we still had some blackberry cordial

left, and Tish gave him some at once. It calmed him somewhat, although he still remained resentful.

"I came here to do a piece of work," he said, "and what happens? I can't even put on my hat! Look at this bump!"

But he did consent to send the policeman away, and I breathed more freely. It was over the matter of the Coronation that he and Tish finally differed, he insisting that we return to America immediately, and Tish refusing to go.

"I have come through a considerable strain," she said, "and I shall remain. I am entitled to a rest."

"A rest!" he exclaimed violently. "I'd like to bet that you feel better at this minute than I do."

"Nevertheless, I shall remain," Tish stated. "I may not see the Coronation itself, but I shall see as much as possible."

He got up angrily, jammed his hat on his head, yelped, and jerked it off again.

"Then all I can say," he said in a savage voice, "is God save the king."

He slammed out the door, and we realized with a sense of relief that our strange journey was indeed over.

•　　•　　•　　•　　•　　•　　•

Perhaps I would never have written this, but Mr. Ostermaier was in a day or so ago about the next hunt dinner, and this brought it all back to me.

He read me the clue for the ice cream, which was to hang in an old well for coolness.

Three ladies went out to fish one day,
and ended across the sea.
So take a look
Ere you drop your hook
Or you'll meet catastrophe.

Before he left he took out of his pocket a small piece of black cloth and handed it to me.

"I meant to bring it long ago," he said, "but I always forgot. Perhaps the young man who—er—lost it might need it."

I gazed at it thoughtfully.

"Not now," I said. "But there was a time when he needed more than that."

TISH
MARCHES ON

TISH MARCHES ON

I

IT WAS shortly after our return from England that Mrs. Ostermaier asked Tish if she would read a paper on the Coronation before the Ladies' Missionary Society. I saw Aggie turn pale, but Tish remained imperturbable, stating merely that she saw little or nothing of it and preferred not to remember what she saw.

The incident, however, recalled to me with great force the events of our stay in London following our strange journey there by dirigible, and in all fairness to Tish I think they should be explained. Especially perhaps the situation when, all being over, we were confronted at Scotland Yard not only by Inspector Jewkes but later on by Tish's own nephew, Charlie Sands.

The Inspector especially looked extremely grim, with the plaster on his lip. He accused us of having abducted and imprisoned him, which was the sheerest nonsense, and actually had the temerity to call us a bunch of wildcats.

Tish was magnificently calm under the accusation. She listened as patiently as she could until he had finished. Then:

"Fiddlesticks," she said tartly, "why on earth

would we kidnap you? I cannot think of anybody I would want less."

The Commissioner, or whoever it was behind the desk, glanced at Mr. Jewkes and smiled.

"Well, well, Jewkes," he said, "you see how it is. These ladies did not want you. Are you sure about this kidnaping?"

"Kidnaping and assault," said the Inspector heavily. "When I came to myself, they were getting ready to hit me again. If you'll look at my lip—"

"Yes, yes, Jewkes," said the Commissioner hastily, "I've seen it already. Still the American sense of humor, Jewkes—"

"If you think it funny, sir," began the Inspector, breathing hard. But the Commissioner merely coughed and looked at us.

"Not funny," he observed mildly, "but still it has its aspects, Jewkes. It has its aspects."

It was then that Charlie Sands came in. He gave a start when he saw us, and I must say that I do not blame him. As usual Tish, in spite of her policeman's uniform, maintained her dignity. But poor Aggie's costume—that of an Indian rajah—was dripping, and now and then she sneezed plaintively. As for me, although I had left the handcart, I found myself still clutching my street broom, and as Charlie Sands stood staring, the Inspector pointed to it.

"That's the weapon they used, sir," he said bitterly. "Plain murderous they are, and that's the fact."

It was after that that Charlie Sands said he did not know us! I saw Tish stiffen, but he refused to look at her.

"It is true," he said, "that they bear a faint—a very faint—resemblance to an aunt of mine and her friends. But no aunt of mine would masquerade as a police officer, assault an inspector of Scotland Yard, or—if I am correctly informed—deliberately imprison a group of fellow Americans."

Tish eyed him.

"Don't be a fool, Charlie," she said sharply. "I could explain everything if that idiot of an inspector would stop talking and give me a chance."

He looked startled at that, and took a more careful survey of us. Then he leaned heavily on the desk and shook his head, as if to clear it.

"The voice," he said, "is familiar; also I seem to have heard the same or similar statements before. It is possible, gentlemen, that I do know these persons. But I wish to go on record here and now as having no responsibility for them. I do not know how they obtained the costumes they are wearing. I do not know how the Inspector obtained that plaster on his face. And what is more," he continued, "I do not want to know. I refuse to know."

He then observed that he was going out to get a drink, or indeed several drinks; and he did go, leaving us there helpless in a foreign land.

The Coronation was over by that time. Large and jubilant crowds filled the streets, and the crown jewels were presumably safe after all. But there we sat, friendless and alone, listening to the slow drip of Aggie's sodden garments and the heavy and infuriated breathing of Inspector Jewkes.

It was indeed a tragic anticlimax.

In a previous account I have related how, through a pure inadvertence, we reached England, having crossed the Atlantic in the *Snark,* a small dirigible belonging to a Mr. Smith; and that it was wrecked on a golf course in Sussex. Also that the police were still searching for us, although it was pure accident that the frying pan had struck a village constable on the head.

We had merely thrown it out, along with other movable articles, in order to lighten the airship. That the constable was below was certainly no fault of ours.

Nevertheless, Tish was determined to stay on and witness the Coronation, although our freedom was greatly circumscribed.

"I have never been afraid of the police yet," she observed, "and I do not intend to start now. Also, I believe that Scotland Yard has been greatly overrated. The way they stop work for meals and tea, as shown in books about them, is actually shameful."

I must say that Aggie, still unnerved by her experience on the target, protested; but in the end we took a small service flat near Piccadilly and settled down as best we could.

We were not uncomfortable, although it was gray and cold. The English turn off all heat early in the spring, regardless of temperature, and Aggie greatly missed her red flannel petticoat, still, I believe, on exhibition at the British Admiralty. And then, only a few days before the Coronation, Tish looked up from the morning paper and said calmly:

"I see that Mr. Smith has arrived."

"Oh, Tish!" Aggie wailed. "What will he do to us?"

"Nothing, unless he finds us," Tish replied. "He has come to salvage the *Snark*."

"Then he's a lunatic," said Aggie violently. "Anybody who wants that thing is raving crazy."

Nevertheless, I was uneasy, and I could see that even Tish was not too happy. The *Daily Mail* had an article entitled: "Claims American Women Stole Dirigible," stating that Mr. Smith had asked Scotland Yard to locate us. Tish read it aloud:

> "It is Mr. Smith's belief that the women are either Communists or hardened criminals, and that at least one is an experienced pilot. Fortunately he brought with him a small photograph of the three, taken on the field by one of the mechanics, and the authorities have widely distributed it. A copy will be found on page eleven of this issue."

Judge of our feelings when, on turning to page eleven, we saw ourselves there! True, we were encumbered with tackle, baskets, and so on. But the resemblance was undoubted, and it was evident that our safety was at an end. Nor were matters helped by a brief letter in the *Times* that same day, which is before me now.

> "Evidently the invasion of England by American criminals has commenced. In this connection it should be remembered that the crown jewels are no longer in the

Tower, and that their value is incalculable.
It would be well to know what steps, if any,
the police have taken to protect them."

As all of us are members in good standing of our
church, and as Tish has taught the same Sunday-
school class for almost forty years, it was quite
dreadful thus to be classed among the enemies of society. Even, as Tish observed, to be virtually prisoners, while all of London and even England was on
the streets, looking at the decorations on Selfridge's
store and so on; or gazing up at the flags and bunt-
ing which carried the letters G.E. and which at first
we thought referred to General Electric, although
actually the initials of the King and Queen.

Then one day, less than a week before the Coronation, Tish insisted upon going to the British Museum
to read up about the crown jewels, and she did not
come back until the next morning!

We were quite frantic, but we dared not go to the
police; when at last she appeared she was in a very
bad humor, having been obliged to spend the night
in the ladies' washroom at the Museum.

"It was that dreadful Smith," she said. "He followed me. He even tried to follow me *there*."

She then asked for a cup of tea, and over it she explained. She said he was not positive of her identity
or he would have called the police. But he had had
the plain indecency to stand outside the washroom
door until the Museum closed, and she herself was
locked in for the night.

All in all we were most uneasy, and it was at this

time that we all cut our hair and had it dyed black.
I must say that it changed us, so that we all felt
safer; but it gave Tish a sinister expression quite
unlike her usual kindly self. Indeed Charlie Sands,
coming in that night, pretended not to know any of
us.

"Sorry, ladies," he said. "Must have got the wrong
floor." He then inspected us more closely and exclaimed, "Holy mackeral! What have you done?"

"We are disguised," said Tish.

"Disguised? You are ruined!" he insisted.

When he heard Tish's story he understood, however, and merely asked us to turn out the lights so
he could not see us. But it was when he was depart-
ing that he made the statement that caused us so
much trouble later.

"You may be safe from Mr. Smith," he said, "but
my advice is to keep away from the police. They
would arrest you on sight, and while I know little
or nothing of English prisons, I gather that they
sadly lack the club spirit to be found in ours at
home."

I could see that Tish was annoyed.

"Why on earth would they arrest us?" she inquired stiffly.

"Because there's a story along Fleet Street today
that a band of American crooks has an eye on the
Kohinoor and other crown jewels. And if ever I saw
a murderous lot of cutthroats I am looking at them
now."

He left on that, and Tish was very quiet during
the remainder of the evening.

Who would have thought that it was to be our last peaceful time for days to come? We had never even heard of Inspector Jewkes. The group of young American men in the flat overhead were merely visitors like ourselves, although sending down for beer at all hours of the day and night. None of us had ever been inside of Madame Tussaud's. And the name Bettina Pell meant nothing to us.

II

It is curious, I think, that we were to meet the Pell girl that very night, and under most unusual circumstances.

Although it was still several days until the Coronation, the celebration had already commenced. Service in our building was practically suspended, the head porter was almost never around, nobody seemed to go to bed, and a Scotch bagpiper that evening chose the pavement beneath our window to make the most dismal sounds.

As a result we did not hear the noises outside our door until very late. Then Tish aroused Aggie and myself, and we investigated. The building had an automatic elevator, or lift, and it was apparently stuck below our floor. Not only this, but a girl inside it was alternately hammering and shouting.

Clad in our dressing gowns, we at once went out. The lift was dark, but we could see her there, evidently in a terrible temper.

"What is the trouble?" Tish inquired.

The girl stopped hammering and looked up.

"Nothing," she said, "nothing at all. I'm here because I like it. I like shouting and yelling and breaking my finger nails on these bars. It's just my way of amusing myself."

Well, we saw at once that she was an American, and that something must be done.

"Have you pressed the button?" Tish inquired.

"Listen," said the girl, "I've pressed everything but flowers for the last hour. And that damned hall porter is out on the street making whoopee somewhere. Get me out of here, can't you?"

It was obviously impossible to leave her there, and at last, the top of the cage being open, we tied some sheets together and with considerable effort drew her to our landing. She was still indignant, however, maintaining that she had been deliberately shut in, and that if somebody named Jim Carlisle thought he was being funny he could think again.

We took her into our sitting room to rest, and seen in the light she was extremely pretty. But I saw her inspecting us with a rather startled expression.

"Not in any trouble yourselves, are you?" she inquired.

Aggie sneezed, but Tish was her usual calm self.

"Certainly not. Why?" she asked.

"I just wondered," she said evasively. "The—the hair is unusual. That's all. Not that it's any of my business, of course."

She then told us her story, maintaining that the power in the lift had been deliberately shut off to keep her a prisoner. She had, she said, had a quarrel with the Carlisle man who lived on the floor above.

and he had shut her up in the lift and left her there.

"He's an unspeakable brute," she said furiously, and then began to cry.

It was some time before she was quiet. Then she explained. She was a newspaperwoman from New York named Bettina Pell, and she had come over to report the Coronation.

"From the woman's point of view," she said. "You know, clothes and jewels. Especially the crown jewels. Then tonight I got a hot tip that they were being moved to Buckingham Palace, and if it had not been for that bunch of thugs on the floor above I'd have had the scoop of the world. If those bandits think they were smart—"

"Bandits!" said Tish. "Actual bandits?"

"I'll tell the world!" she said. "They'll steal, rob, and probably murder to get what they're after. They'll—oh, what's the use," she finished drearily. "I'm going home to bed. Not that it's much of a home. I'm sleeping in a bathtub at the moment. And thanks for the lift, which isn't a bad pun at this hour of the night."

It was when she was leaving that I saw her glance at that wretched newspaper picture of us, and I thought she looked startled. But she went away without comment, and Tish voiced our general feeling about her.

"It is very sad," she said, "that one so young should consort with any gang. But I believe such men often have a fatal attraction for the other sex. To have locked her in that elevator was sheer brutality."

She was thoughtful, saying little after that; and it was not until three A.M. that Aggie roused me from a sound sleep to report that she was not in her room. What is more, only her bathrobe and slippers were missing, and when it became apparent that our dear Tish was somewhere in the cold London night, unclothed and possibly in danger, our state of mind was quite dreadful.

It was almost dawn when at last we heard a commotion in the bathroom, and discovered her climbing in the window from the fire escape. She closed the window, shivered slightly, and then confronted us.

"That girl was right," she said grimly. "Those men above *are* bandits. I have no doubt whatever that they intend to secure the crown jewels; if indeed they have not already done so."

She said nothing more until we had made her a cup of tea. Iron woman as she is, she had passed through a dreadful ordeal, and it was some time before she had quite recovered.

"There can be no doubt whatever," she then explained. "The place is littered with cases containing machine guns, and the ammunition is in round tins in a closet. I had to sit on it. Not only that," she added: "the raid is to be made at the Coronation itself. And the Master Mind is in America!"

Well, it was a long story, although a terrible one. She had been unable to sleep, and had gone up the fire escape to inspect the rooms above by looking through a window. The gang being out, she had climbed in, to make the discoveries I have mentioned. But here misfortune overtook her. They came back before she could escape, and she had been forced to find refuge in a closet!

It was due to this that she heard the cable message, however. The one the others called Jim Carlisle read it aloud to the rest.

"Listen to this, gang," he said. "It's from New York. From the boss."

And then he read the most bloodcurdling message I have ever heard. It said:

> BE SURE NO MISTAKE ABOUT LOCATIONS.
> ESPECIALLY WANT JEWELS AND DECORA-
> TIONS. BETTER NOT SHOOT UNTIL YOU CAN
> SEE THE WHITES OF THEIR EYES.

We were too horrified for speech. Tish finished her tea and put down her cup.

"There is but one thing to do," she said, "dangerous as it may be I feel that we have no alternative. We must go to Scotland Yard at once."

Aggie immediately protested, but Tish was firm. And I think it should be said in our defense that we did so that same morning. Nothing was printed in the London press to this effect. Indeed, nothing in our defense was ever printed at all, and as it turned out the risk was entirely useless. The Commissioner who saw us—I think that was his title—seemed to be very busy, and on Tish stating her errand, he merely raised his eyebrows and addressed a large man who was standing by.

"You might get me the plot file, Jewkes," he said.

And when Jewkes had gone he turned to Tish.

"We have a number of plots just now," he said.

"The natural anxiety of a loyal people to protect—er —the royal jewels and so on. About two thousand, I fancy." He then took a large file from Mr. Jewkes, and examined it. "Yes," he went on, "one thousand nine hundred and ninety-eight. Good guess, that; eh, Jewkes?"

"Very good, sir," said Mr. Jewkes.

I could see that Tish was annoyed.

"These people have machine guns and ammunition," she said rather sharply. "If that interests you."

"It does indeed. Excellent weapons; eh, Jewkes? First time we've had machine guns reported, I believe. Let's see. Yes. Bombs, grenades, rifles, and I believe a brick or two. But—"

Here Tish rose with dignity.

"Would you be interested—even faintly—in knowing the headquarters of this gang?" she demanded

"Oh, rather," he said. "We haven't much to do just now; have we, Jewkes? There are only about fifteen million people in town, but we'll take the address. Naturally. Put it down, Jewkes."

And it was after this had been done that we had a very narrow escape. A man opened the door and said:

"The American about the dirigible, sir."

"Show him into the other room," said the Commissioner resignedly, "and get the dirigible file. What does he expect me to do about his blooming balloon anyhow? Blow it up for him?"

It was Mr. Smith!

III

Fortunately he did not see us, although I must say that I was nervous when we reached the street. Tish, however, was calm. As is usual when she is revolving some course in her mind, outside and petty irritations meant nothing to her.

"It is evident," she said at last, "that we can expect no help from the police. Whatever is done we must do ourselves."

"Do what?" I inquired. "This gang has done nothing as yet."

"We must prevent their doing anything, Lizzie," she said quietly.

And this, I think, should be borne in mind as I record the events that followed. Scotland Yard had failed us and, except for the subsequent involvement of Inspector Jewkes, did nothing whatever; and Tish's idea all along was that an ounce of prevention was worth a pound of cure.

Curiously enough, the Carlisle man was at the porter's desk when we went back, and he did not resemble a gangster at all. He was tall and quite good-looking, and he was asking if anybody had found a young lady in the elevator the night before.

"What young lady was that, sir?"

"Did you see her?" the Carlisle man demanded, looking angry.

"No, sir. There was a young lady went out, I don't know just when. Seemed kind of upset about something. Slammed the door like to break the glass out of it."

"What time was that?" he inquired.

"About three hours after you left, sir."

Well, I thought he was going to leap over the desk at the porter, and Aggie gasped beside me. But he controlled himself.

"And where were you, all that time?" he said, in a cold rage. And added: "Did it ever occur to you that someday one of us might take you for a ride and just lose you by the wayside?"

Yes, he said that. Mild and handsome as he looked, we all three knew the awful gangster threat in his words. But the porter merely smiled.

"Yes, sir. Thank you, sir," he said.

We were all considerably unnerved when we reached our flat. Surprised also, for when we opened the door Bettina Pell was in the sitting room.

She was lying on the couch smoking a cigarette, and she sat up and grinned at us.

"Sorry!" she said. "If you'd spent the night in a bathtub you'd understand."

She then got up and looked us all over carefully, and to my dismay I saw that she had that wretched newspaper picture in her hand.

"What a break!" she said, as though to herself. "Oh, what a break!" Then she said briskly. "All right. Let's sit down and you tell mamma all about it."

"About what?" Tish inquired.

"You know," she said. "All about the *Snark* and the flannel petticoat, and trying to kill the constable, and the man you hung on the church steeple. You

haven't told anybody else, have you?" she asked
anxiously.

I can remember that Aggie gave a low moan, and
that that wretched girl actually got out a notebook
and pencil and sat smiling at us. As Tish said later,
she was certainly dangerous, loaded with information as she was, and ready to explode if pointed in
the wrong direction. It was a deadly situation: on
the one hand, Mr. Smith and our probable arrest;
on the other, a dastardly plot, so shocking that we
needed our freedom to foil it.

But I had forgotten our resolute Tish, so quick
to think in times of danger. She had taken off her
hat, and now she sat down and picked up her knitting.

"The *Snark?*" she inquired, "What on earth is the
Snark?"

Bettina stared at her.

"It won't do, Miss Carberry," she said coolly. "If
that is your attitude—"

"It is my attitude at the moment," Tish replied
with firmness. "I may, I just possibly may, alter it
later. That, however, depends upon you."

The girl seemed surprised. She put down her pencil and sat back.

"All right," she said, "I get you. Let's have it."

Well, I watched Bettina Pell while Tish told in
detail of her discoveries the night before, and if ever
I saw a girl thunderstruck it was she. At one time—
I believe when Tish told her of the cable—she even
burst into hysterical laughter. But at the end she
was calm enough.

"Let's get this straight," she said. "They haven't done anything, so that's out. But they're going to do something, so that's in. The general idea being—"

"The general idea," said Tish, putting down her knitting, "is to put them beyond trouble until all is over and the crown jewels and so on are safe once more. A good cellar, or a dungeon in fair repair, would answer."

But here, I regret to state, Bettina became hysterical again.

"In a—in a dungeon!" she gasped. "Down in a dungeon deep! I wish I could see their faces when it happens. And where is the dungeon? Don't tell me you haven't got a dungeon."

"As a matter of fact I have," said Tish astonishingly. "At least it was there many years ago, and I dare say it still is."

Bettina stared at her, almost with awe.

"It must be true," she said. "I'm awake. I'm not dreaming. And she has a dungeon. You—you couldn't give me a cup of tea, could you? I feel rather gone."

The rest of her visit was occupied with details. We needed her assistance, Tish said, and in return for it she was to have the full story of our adventures on the *Snark,* not to be used, of course, until we were safely out of England and on the way home. Bettina agreed to all this, and was in high spirits as she prepared to depart.

"You get the dungeon," she said gaily. "And I'll do the rest."

"How will you do it?" Tish inquired.

"That is my secret," she said, and refused any further explanation.

She went away soon after, and apparently the hysteria returned, for on looking out the window I saw her standing on the pavement wiping her eyes, and several passers-by glanced at her curiously.

I can write calmly of her now, but there was a time when I could not mention her name. Pretty and young, she deliberately used us as the agents of a petty revenge; and almost destroyed Charlie Sands in so doing. But perhaps we should have known. I still remember how she flushed when Tish asked if her affections were engaged with any member of the gang.

"Affections!" she said. "Listen. When I think of what they did to me last night I make Vesuvius look like a ripe boil. But don't you worry about me," she added. "I'll get even with Jim Carlisle if it's the last thing I ever do."

Yes, perhaps we should have known.

IV

That was on the Saturday preceding the Coronation. Tish had rented a car and spent the afternoon locating the castle she had remembered; while Aggie and I remained at home, keeping a keen eye on the stairs and elevator. Thus we saw diverse members of the gang at intervals, and both of us were impressed with their youth and cheerfulness, in spite of their bloodthirsty business.

Indeed, they whistled both coming and going, although the Carlisle man seemed rather depressed. Once or twice he rang a telephone number and asked for Bettina—as we now called her—but with no success, and we distinctly heard him kick a chair after one such failure.

Then late that afternoon we saw Inspector Jewkes go up to their flat, and waited with bated breath for possible trouble. All that happened, however, was that after ten minutes or so a boy carried up beer on a tray, and there was considerable laughter to be heard when the door was opened.

But it was when he departed that the horrifying thing occurred. He stood in the hall just over our heads, and we both heard him clearly as he said good-bye.

"Well, all right, boys," he said. "And remember, don't shoot until you see the whites of their eyes."

He was laughing as he passed our door!

We told Tish when she returned, but she merely shrugged her shoulders. She had located the dungeon, only twenty miles from London, and said that one extra—such as the Inspector—would make no difference whatever.

"It is quite large," she said, "also dry and sanitary. And the caretaker is entirely deaf."

In other words, she said, we could hold the entire band of criminals there safe until the danger was past. But she also added that blankets and food should be provided; and in this connection a strange thing happened to us that very night.

We had done our buying, and were returning with our arms piled high, when that wretched lift stuck again with all of us inside. The hall porter was gone as usual, and for some hours we could do nothing but wait.

It was the bandits who rescued us!

They came in singing noisily at two A.M., and after pressing the button started to walk up the stairs. As these wound around the wire enclosure that housed the elevator, we were plainly visible, and the one we knew as Jim Carlisle stopped and stared.

"Hello!" he said. "What's happened?"

Aggie gave a low moan of terror, but Tish preserved her equanimity.

"We are quite all right," she said. "Please go on and leave us alone."

"See here," he said, looking surprised. "You don't mean that you like it there?"

The rest had all stopped, and it was an eerie feeling, surrounded as we were by them and entirely helpless. But there was nothing to be done. The Carlisle man turned to the others and said: "Well, fellows, how about it?" and in a short time we were released once more.

Not only that! They insisted on our going up to their rooms, and refused to take any denial.

Aggie was visibly trembling by this time; seeing this, they mixed for each of us a glass of tonic, consisting of something smelling like creosote and an effervescent water. It was most effective, but for some reason it upset Aggie, who had taken cold while in the elevator. She got up and then sat down suddenly.

"There's ad earthquake!" she said. "The roob's moving!"

"That's all right, sister," said the Carlisle man. "Hold tight and all will be well."

"I'b used to holdig tight," she said. "All the way across the the Atlatic—"

Fortunately she sneezed at that moment, and Tish rose abruptly.

"She is tired and not herself," she observed. "I shall take her down and—"

But here Aggie laughed, quite a hysterical laugh.

"Dowd, dowd, id the dudgeod deep," she said, swaying slightly. "Ad let go of be, Tish. I wadt to see the bachide guds."

It was one of the worst moments of my life, but the Carlisle man merely smiled.

"Trot out the tommy-gun for the lady, Joe," he said to one of the others.

It was bloodcurdling to see them laugh over this, and Tish and I managed finally to get Aggie downstairs and put her to bed, with no worse results than a bad headache the next morning.

That was Sunday, and since we could not go to church, Tish spent the time checking her lists for our prisoners. It was that day that I saw Mr. Smith from the window and was obliged to beat a hasty retreat. He did not see me, however. He was walking along slowly, looking at the people as they passed with searching eyes, and I must say I felt uncomfortable.

I told Tish, but she merely regarded me vaguely.

"Don't bother me, Lizzie," she said. "Now let me

see: bottled water, blankets, bread, candles and matches, sardines, can opener—"

"It sounds like a picnic," I said. "A bloodthirsty lot of ruffians, and you coddle them like a Sunday-school excursion."

She was busy adding oranges to the list—because of the vitamins, I believe—and paid no attention.

There was only one other incident that day worth noting, but it showed me how narrow was our margin of safety.

The sitting-room door was open, and I heard Bettina's high heels as she came up the stairs. She stopped outside our door, and with that the Carlisle wretch hurled himself down and put his arms around her.

"Bettina darling!" he said. "Kiss and make up, won't you?"

She was weakening. I could see it in her face. And he kept on. He said he was sorry. He said he would get down and let her walk all over him. He said she could lock him in a dozen elevators. And indeed I do not know what would have been the end had she not seen me. I dare say that reminded her of what she had at stake, for she pushed him away suddenly and told him not to bother her.

"Bother!" he said. "What do you mean, bother?"

"Just what it sounds like. Or I can spell it for you."

"And that's all?"

"That's enough, isn't it?"

"I'm to scram?"

"You're to scram."

Puzzling as this language was, he at least understood it. He stood quite still. Then he took her by the shoulders, gave her a good shaking, and turned and went upstairs again, whistling. It was precisely the way gangsters treat their sweethearts in the pictures, and I was not surprised to see tears in her eyes when she came in.

"The great hulking brute," she said stormily. "I'll get even with him if it's the last thing I ever do."

Nevertheless, she did not let sentiment interfere with business. It was that day that she got Tish to sign an agreement with her; that agreement which she was to use with such duplicity later. It read:

> In return for services rendered I hereby agree to give the exclusive story of our adventures on the Snark to Miss Bettina Pell and no one else. (Signed) Letitia Carberry.

It was the next night, Monday, that we locked up the criminals.

The affair passed without incident. We reached the castle at dusk, and no caretaker being in sight, Tish led us at once to the dungeon. Here we left our supplies, and Tish carefully oiled the lock and the hinges of the door. Then, leaving a lighted candle, as Bettina had suggested, we retreated behind some fallen masonry and waited.

I must say I was highly nervous, and to add to my anxiety the damp at once affected Aggie, who began to sneeze violently. It therefore seemed a long time before we heard a car, and an even longer one before, led by flashlights, the gang appeared. The Carlisle man was in the lead, and he soon observed the light.

"This seems to be it," he said. "All right, you fellows. Got the equipment?"

In the darkness I peered out, and I could see that the others were laden with the gun cases and so on. To my horror one of them was already opening one of them. But this was nothing to what followed. A large heavy man stepped forward and peered into the room, and I could hardly believe my eyes.

It was Inspector Jewkes!

We were greatly startled, but it was too late to draw back. When they were all inside Tish hastily slammed the heavy door and locked it; and there was a shocking uproar inside at once. I think even Tish was unnerved.

It was not until we were on our way back to London, however, that she explained.

"That man Jewkes saw me, Lizzie," she said. "And if there was ever murder in a man's face it was in his."

V

None of us slept well that night. I kept hearing a heavy body hurling itself against the dungeon door, and Aggie had a nightmare in which we had hung the Inspector on a church steeple and were firing at him with machine guns. And to make things worse Tish, awakening early, discovered that she had lost the key to the dungeon.

All in all it was a bad morning. And at eleven o'clock that idiot Bettina came and tried to tell us that it was all a joke!

I have never seen Tish so indignant.

"A joke!" she said. "Then all I have to say is that I hope Inspector Jewkes thinks it is funny."

She looked blank.

"Jewkes? Who is he?" she asked.

"He is not a member of the gang?"

"I never heard of him."

"Then I have to tell you," Tish observed quietly, "that through some mistake an inspector from Scotland Yard is locked in with your friends. And as far as I am concerned he will have to stay here."

I shall never forget the look of sheer anguish she gave us.

"Oh, my God!" she said. "That's torn it!"

Nevertheless, the knowledge that the Inspector did not belong to the gang had altered the situation greatly, and after some thought Tish decided to notify the police. But repeated attempts to get the Yard by telephone merely resulted in a weary voice which said:

"Sorry. All applications must be made by mail."

In desperation we finally went to the Yard ourselves that afternoon, and after a long wait we saw the same Commissioner we had seen before. Evidently he remembered us, for he simply looked up and said:

"What! Another plot!"

"The same one," said Tish coldly. "Only I am

happy to report that the gang is now safely locked away."

"That's fine," he said. "Splendid, one less gang, eh? I'd better get the gang file. Jewkes! Where's Jewkes?"

I saw Tish draw a long breath.

"Inspector Jewkes," she said, "is locked away also."

He seemed quite unimpressed. He said absently: "Well, well. Good for old Jewkes. Probably very interesting for him, eh?" Then he picked up the telephone, said "chump chops and chips" into it, and rose.

"Sorry, ladies," he said. "Big day. Coronation tomorrow. Have to trot along now."

He was almost out of the room when Tish confronted him.

"In a dungeon," she stated, "and not having chump chops and chips, either. If that means anything to you."

But he only looked at her vaguely.

"Too bad," he said. "He was fond of them too, poor fellow."

On that he simply went out the door and left us there. And it was on the way home that we unexpectedly saw Mr. Smith.

He was on the top of a taxicab, with an American flag in one hand and a tin horn in another; and every now and then he would yell: "Their majesties, bless their young hearts." Quite a crowd had collected, and he had just started to yell again when his eyes fell on us, and he remained with his mouth open, staring. Then he shouted:

"Here, let me out, I want those women. Police! Police!"

He started to climb down, and Tish at once moved rapidly down the street. But he kept on after us, calling for the police, and at last Tish stepped into a doorway and dragged us in after her.

It was all most unpleasant, especially as he had now almost overtaken us. Fortunately, we discovered in time where we were, and were able to pay our way and enter before he reached us. It was Madame Tussaud's waxworks, and never have I so appreciated Tish's clear thinking as at that moment.

"Mix with the figures," she said. "And stand perfectly still."

It was near closing time and the rooms were almost empty, only a woman with a small boy being near, and thus we were able to dispose of ourselves quickly in the Chamber of Horrors. The lights being dim, my only fear was that Aggie would sneeze. And then that awful child came and stood in front of me, and stared for a long time.

"This lady winked, mother," he said in a loud voice.

"Don't tell me lies, young man," said his mother.

"But she did wink," he persisted, "I saw her."

They were still arguing over this when Mr. Smith came in. He was breathing hard, but after a look he was about to depart when that wretched boy, having moved to Aggie, stuck a toy feather duster in her face. As Aggie is allergic to feathers she sneezed immediately, and Mr. Smith started.

"What was that?" he said in a savage voice.

"Just my little boy," said the woman. "Come here, Reginald, and let mother wipe your nose. He won't wear his jacket, sir, and that's a fact."

"I didn't sneeze," said the little monster. "It was that—"

Here the woman slapped him for telling another falsehood, and at last they all departed, leaving us alone. Somewhere we could hear Mr. Smith insisting that we had come in and that he was staying until we came out again. But as it was already closing time he was obliged to leave, and we could then face our situation.

It was bad indeed. The lights went out almost at once, and soon after the entrance was closed and locked. How can I describe our sensations, left alone in that weird spot, with the lifelike effigies of dreadful criminals all around us? Nor were matters improved when, after making a reconnaissance, Tish reported that Mr. Smith was still outside the entrance and that he was talking to a constable. Also that some cleaners had appeared, and we could not long hope to remain undiscovered.

Rarely have I put in such a night. The constable never moved, and to add to our misery was the fact that soon the Coronation would commence and that, after all we had endured, we would not see it.

But I had counted without Tish, and at three in the morning she came to me with her idea. This was merely to exchange our outer garments for those of various figures near by, preferably male, and thus be able to escape the constable's eye. And this in the end was what we did: Aggie chose those of an Indian potentate in a turban and so on; I donned with some repugnance a street sweeper's outfit, with brush and pan; Tish took the uniform from a policeman who had murdered his wife.

This, I think, fully explains our costumes on the morning of the Coronation; and the necessity which drove us to them. It also explains the terrified shrieks from one of the charwomen, and her statement to the press later.

"Of course I screamed," she said. "What would you 'ave done? I looked up from my pail and there was those three bloody murderers as I 'ave dusted for fifteen years, coming at me in a row."

It was gray dawn when we reached the street. As no taxis or cars were allowed, it was already jammed with people, and with great relief we lost ourselves among them; Tish observing that having done our duty we could now look forward to a bath and breakfast, and later to the Coronation itself with peaceful minds.

But it was not to be. When we approached our building we saw Charlie Sands outside talking to the hall porter. He seemed in a frenzy of rage, and we heard him clear across the street.

"But damn it, man," he shouted, "when did they go? And where?"

"That would be the night before last, sir," said

the porter. "As to where, that I couldn't say. They had an inspector from Scotland Yard along, that's all I know."

Well, he looked stupefied, and just then a most astonishing thing happened. Dirty and unshaven, the Carlisle man came running up the street, followed by the rest of the gang, and Charlie Sands gave him a furious look and said:

"Where the hell have you been?"

"Someday," said the Carlisle man, grinning, "when I've got a long, long time to spare, I'll tell you."

Tish said nothing. I could see her marching on, in that dreadful uniform, and I merely followed her.

I do not know just where we lost Aggie, although as events turned out, it was probably near Buckingham Palace. I do not know where some unidentified man thrust a street cleaner's cart before me and told me to get a move on, or words to that effect. I do recall most vividly that when we went into a public washroom to perform our morning ablutions we were put out angrily by a red-faced woman, who asked us if we had no decency.

But I do know when and where we saw Aggie again. It must have been eleven o'clock by that time, and what with Tish's ominous silence and pushing the cart ahead of me, I was dropping on my feet. Then the crowd around us began to cheer, and we saw that we were on the route of march. The gold coach went by, with the young King and Queen inside, for all the world like fairy-tale royalty, and following them came the King's Indian guard.

On a horse among them, and looking completely agonized, was our unfortunate friend!

How can I record our feelings! Every now and then the horse turned its head and took a nip at Aggie's leg. And then, even as we watched, the tragedy occurred. A mounted band struck up close by, and that horse simply lifted his head, whirled, and bolted down a side street with Aggie clinging helplessly to his back.

To our bewilderment was now added anxiety, and we spent the remainder of the morning searching for our beloved companion. It was, I think, in Kensington Gardens that Tish's keen eyes at last saw a horse quietly grazing on the bank of the Round Pond, and a moment later we saw Aggie.

To our amazement she was standing in the water up to her waist, and behaving in a most peculiar manner. She would stand for a moment, take a firm grip on her nose and then disappear entirely. This she repeated several times; nor did she desist when we approached the bank.

It was indeed some time before she even noticed us. Then she sneezed several times and said in a tragic voice:

"I'be losth theb agaid."

"Lost what?" said Tish.

"By teeth," she replied, and dived once more.

She discovered them at last and, as she was both lame and completely exhausted, we placed her in my cart and started for home.

On the way she told her painful story. Stripped of the coryza which afflicts her at such times, it was quite simple. She had merely, on losing us, wandered about until she found herself outside the gate of Buckingham Palace. Here, to her surprise, an excited-looking man in black satin knee breeches had seen her and led her inside.

There she found a number of Indian rajahs and so on, dressed much as she was; and before she knew it someone was holding a horse in front of her and telling her to get on.

The rest, alas, we knew.

VI

That is really the end of my record, and I do not believe that Tish was greatly surprised when, on reaching home, we found Inspector Jewkes waiting for us inside.

He was red with fury, and with a roar he rushed forward and caught Tish by the arm.

"Well, madam," he said ferociously, "you have had your little joke. Now I will have mine."

But he did not have it just then. Undoubtedly Tish was in an extremely nervous state, although usually the mildest of women. His onslaught apparently startled her, and with a jerk she tore my street broom from my hand and threatened him with it.

He ran straight into it, and we were all astonished to see him fall down and lie still.

This is the so-called "Brutal Attack On Scotland Yard Inspector," but the whole idea is preposterous.

Nor did we cut him on the lip, as reported. He, himself, struck the fender as he dropped.

As for saying that we were preparing to attack him again when he recovered consciousness, I have never heard such nonsense. Aggie's action in seizing the poker was pure self defense.

But it was a comfort, on being taken to Scotland Yard, to find ourselves facing the same commissioner as before. He seemed amused about something, and he surveyed the Inspector's lip with interest.

"Injuries received in the line of duty, Jewkes?" he inquired.

"Knocked down by these women—if they *are* women, in those clothes!" the Inspector snarled. "And a fine bunch of wildcats they are, sir. First I'm locked up in a damp cellar and then I'm attacked. They'd be put away for life, if I had my way."

"Tut, tut," said the Commissioner. "We have to allow for the American sense of humor, Jewkes."

The Inspector fairly swelled with rage.

"All I can say, sir—if you think it's funny—"

The Commissioner looked at us and coughed.

"Well, it has its aspects, Jewkes," he said. "It has its aspects."

But at last we were able to tell the Commissioner our story, from first to last, and he seemed much interested. Indeed, he said that it sounded better than fiction.

"Not often we get such things here," he said.

"Very drab life usually. Very drab." Then he brightened. "So you locked old Jewkes up! Do him good probably. Get pretty well fed up with him myself."

Also sometime during that interval they brought in Mr. Smith, and asked him if he knew us. He seemed literally to swell with rage.

"Know them!" he shouted. "Do I know them! Listen, I've been chasing them from New Jersey and the Atlantic Ocean to somebody's waxworks. They stole the best blimp ever built, and now it's beyond hope. Gone, destroyed!"

"Oh," said the Commissioner with an air of relief. "Then you don't expect me to blow it up for you."

But the really important incident occurred when they brought in Bettina Pell. She went quite pale when she saw us, and also when she looked at the Inspector's lip. It was, however, what she said that left us thunderstruck.

"Jim Carlisle had played a nasty trick on me," she said, in a small voice. "So I wanted to get even. It was—well, it was really a joke."

"You get that, Jewkes?" said the Commissioner. "The American sense of humor again. Eh, what?"

"I got it, right enough," said Inspector Jewkes grimly.

Bettina looked frightened.

"That's all," she said. "I only meant to shut them up overnight and give them a scare. I'd told them that the women from the *Snark* were hiding there, and I showed them an agreement signed by Miss Carberry. So they went, and—well, that's all."

She then began to cry, and said that we had taken matters into our own hands and locked up Inspector Jewkes too. And that we had lost the key, and anyhow she couldn't let them out or the Inspector would have arrested her.

"And I had my Coronation piece to do," she said. The Commissioner looked interested again.

"Ah," he said. "So they lost the key, eh? Then how the devil *did* you get out, Jewkes?"

Then we saw the Inspector smile for the first and only time.

"The ladies had left us a can opener," he said.

Well, as I have said, that is really all of the story. Save for one thing. Late that afternoon Charlie Sands appeared, and after looking us over, disclaimed us entirely. But I find that I omitted what he said before he departed.

"Not today," he said, "but sometime, when I am feeling stronger, I want to hear just why you locked up my camera crew and damned near ruined me."

That, I think, completes the record. We were released that evening, but we had great difficulty in getting back into our flat, the head porter at first refusing to admit us. When at last he recognized us he leered most unpleasantly.

"Look as though you'd been 'aving a night out, not 'alf," he said.

Tish was very silent that night, but how thankful we were to get out of those terrible clothes, and having bathed, to sit quietly over a cup of hot tea. But we did not go to bed. The noise overhead prohibited it.

We were sitting by the fire, Tish knitting and Aggie with her feet in a hot mustard foot bath, when we heard the door open overhead, and the noise coming down the stairs. It was apparently all the crowd from above, and it was singing: "Hail, hail, the gang's all here."

I tried to close the door, but it was too late. They were already coming into the room, and to our amazement Inspector Jewkes and the Carlisle man had Bettina Pell by the arms. They shoved her forward and then stood back.

"All right," said Mr. Carlisle. "Now, my girl, make your little speech."

I must say she looked very pretty, although rather scared. But she stepped forward and said:

"I'm sorry, I'm frightfully sorry for getting you into trouble. And—"

There she stopped, and the Carlisle man prompted her. "And I promise—"

"And I promise never to do it again."

"Go on," said Mr. Carlisle.

She swallowed hard.

"I am a mean and vindictive person. I have no professional ethics and no sense of decency. And I—I forget the rest of it, Jim."

"No, you don't," he said firmly. "Get on with it."

"And I promise to be a good girl hereafter so that Jim Carlisle may marry me someday."

"Right," said the Carlisle man. And with that they all turned solemnly and went up the stairs again. . . .

It seems a long time now since all that happened.

It turned out that Mr. Smith's dirigible was insured, and the case never came to trial. But now and then I have dreams, when I see Aggie so mysteriously holding her nose and diving into the Round Pond. Or Tish, marching on in her policeman's uniform, while I trundle that awful cart before me.

But my real nightmare is of standing rigid in Madame Tussaud's waxworks, and hearing that wretched little boy bleat:

"This lady winked, mother."

Now and then Charlie Sands comes in for a glass of our blackberry cordial, and only the other night he observed that Bettina had just been married. We were not surprised, but Tish remarked that she hoped she would make a good wife.

"He was a good-looking man," she said thoughtfully. "And he was firm. I am sure that she needs firmness."

Charlie Sands stared at her.

"Who on earth are you talking about?" he inquired.

"Didn't you say she had married Jim Carlisle?"

"I didn't say," he observed dryly. "As a matter of fact she married Jewkes."

That is all. But the other day I was helping Tish to clean out her desk and came across a small slip of paper. It was a list, and it read as follows: Bottled water, blankets, bread, candles, matches, sardines, and can opener.

I looked at Tish, but she had not noticed it; and so, unseen, I was able to throw it away.

THE MOUSE

THE MOUSE

I

ONLY THE other day our dear Tish observed that the attempt to help humanity was always an ungrateful one. To support this she quoted the incident of the mouse, and the attitude of Charlie Sands, her nephew, when he found her tied to the bed in the psychopathic ward of our local hospital. She had been on the board of that hospital for years, but no one had even recognized her. As to Charlie Sands himself, his manner was cold and even resentful when, having at last discovered her, he stood over her bed and gazed down at her.

"What does this mean?" was his opening speech, in a stern voice. "Open your eyes and look at me. *What* about an elephant?"

And when she tried to tell him about where she had left Aggie, and about the elephant and so on, the doctor—who should have known better—said that this was merely a delusion. Nor were things better about the peanuts, although that should have been obvious.

"All right," said Charlie Sands. "I get some of it. According to you Aggie has been captured by an elephant and Lizzie has lost her hat. But you are here. What I want to know is why you are here. And how."

"I was merely trying to get some peanuts," said Tish coldly. "What is so extraordinary about that?"

"That is what I am asking," he observed. "The fact that you broke into the stand in the middle of the night to do so is not unusual. Nor even the fact that a police officer claims that you broke his nose. All I am asking is why? Why are you here? And why, for instance, the peanuts?"

And then Tish became her old self, after a night of anxiety and hazard such as few women could have endured.

"Don't be a fool," she said sharply. "For the elephant, of course."

It was I believe at that time that the nurse brought him the aromatic ammonia.

As Tish has said since, it should all have been perfectly clear to him by that time. After all, we had spent the entire night attempting to help him, and that at his own request. As to his observation—made later—that the broken fire plug flooded a number of cellars, all damage has since been paid. And I still maintain that resistance to unjustified capture is a citizen's duty. We have all seen Officer O'Brien since, and if his nose was broken by the rim of the butterfly net it certainly shows no sign of it.

Actually it began with Charlie Sands' request that we find a mouse for him. We had dined with Tish that night, and Hannah, Tish's maid, had baked one of her celebrated pecan-nut pies. What with that and a glass each of blackberry cordial we were in a contented frame of mind. Then the doorbell rang, and it was Charlie Sands, accompanied by a very pretty girl.

It appeared that her name was Paula, and that her father was the managing editor of Charlie Sands' newspaper. Also that she herself did the society column on the paper. But I must admit that we were surprised at the object of their visit.

They wanted a mouse!

"Preferably a live one," said Charlie Sands. "Certainly one of a bland expression, undamaged by the usual sort of trap. A domestic mouse, even a good family mouse, with the usual fangs, whiskers and so on. The taxidermist insists on these."

"What taxidermist?" Tish inquired.

"The one who is going to mount the head," he said.

I dare say we looked bewildered, for Paula hastened to explain. Her father had lately returned from a hunting trip in Africa, bringing a number of trophies, such as mounted heads and antlers. What was more, he talked of nothing else, and something had to be done about it.

"He's driven mother crazy," she said. "You know how it is: zebra rugs, lionskins hither and yon, a stuffed giraffe with a ten-foot neck in the corner, an elephant's foot and leg for an umbrella stand and a hippopotamus over the mantel. And it's as bad at the office. So now we want a mouse."

Tish dropped her knitting and stared at them.

"But why a mouse?" she inquired. "A bushel of moths would be better."

They liked their own plan better, however, the

idea being that all the office force give him a bang-up dinner with speeches, and then present him the head of a mouse, properly mounted. It appeared that he *had* killed a mouse some days before, but had fed it to the office cat.

"It's to be a hint," said Charlie Sands. "A hint that we're fed up, as you may say. But now that we need one we can't find a mouse. How about this building? Does the janitor have mice, or does he keep a cat?"

"He keeps a cat," Tish informed him.

Charlie Sands then gave a hollow groan and said that this was Friday and they had to have the mouse by Monday. Only there were no mice.

"It's a crying evil," he said. "There must be millions of cats about. When I think of all the poor little *Mus musculus*—or whatever the plural is—hounded by millions of cats, it seems both cruel and unfair."

In the end they asked us if we would undertake the commission, all else having failed, and Tish finally agreed. Only Aggie protested, having a terror of the creatures, but Tish ignored her.

"It seems a simple matter," she observed. "We shall need tomorrow to make a few preparations, but that is all."

I remember that Charlie Sands looked rather anxious at that.

"Of course," he said hastily, "what we want is merely a mouse. Not a camel or a tiger. Not even a rhinoceros. Just bear that in mind, will you? Knowing you as I do—"

"I think you can trust me," said Tish coldly, and took up her knitting again.

They were more cheerful after that, and as they prepared to go he swore us to secrecy on the whole matter; especially to watch out for one man.

"One of our fellows got fired the other day," he said. "He disappeared for a week and the old man let him out. He might be dangerous. He knows the plot."

I noticed that Paula colored.

"That idiot!" she said. "What can he do? I wrote him a note asking him to get me a mouse, and he read it moose and went all the way to Canada for it. Was it my fault that it got him into a tree and then tried to butt the tree down?"

However that might be, Charlie Sands warned us to be careful of this person, whose name appeared to be Bill Lawrence, and who, having failed to secure the mouse himself, had flatly stated that no one else would. He had indeed said that he would either be reinstated on the paper or he would publish the whole story in the rival newspaper, the *Gazette*.

"He would do it too," said Paula. "He is angry and capable of anything. Also he has a terrible disposition, mean and vindictive. I am sorry for any girl who is idiot enough to marry him."

She then sighed and said he was no reporter anyhow, and the office was well rid of him; but he had no idea we were going to help them out, and so we were probably safe.

They finally departed, and we went into executive session at once. As Charlie Sands had said, mice were like athlete's foot: many are afflicted but few admit it. And although we are opposed to killing any living creature, all of us being members of the S.P.C.A., there was no doubt that mice carried germs and were therefore a menace to the human race.

It was Tish's suggestion that we make the capture as painless as possible, and that to this end a butterfly net and a pound or so of cheese would be the only essentials.

"In this way," she said, "will the mouse not only be uninjured, but placed at once in a jar with the cheese, its last hours will be happy and its final expression mild and normal."

Our preparations the next day were simple. Tish made out a list, including the butterfly net, a flashlight, a pound of cheese, and a small tin of shoe blacking in case we needed to darken our faces. These we secured. But it became evident after certain inquiries that the search was not to be so simple as we had anticipated.

Hannah, interrogated as to mice in the kitchen, burst into tears and offered to leave at once; and the janitor of Tish's building was most unpleasant.

"Mice!" he said. "There's none there unless you put them there yourself, Miss Carberry. And *that* wouldn't surprise me either," he added darkly.

I must say that Aggie, too, was most discouraging. As fear always affects her nasal passages, she sneezed constantly, so that in the end Tish suggested that she need not participate. This only offended her, although time was to prove that our dear

Tish as usual had been right. I may say, too, that up to that afternoon we had not considered the matter of a mousetrap. As Tish said, with such a contraption we ran the risk of injury to the mouse.

But that afternoon a young man called with quite an unusual one. True, it was large and bulky, but he stated at once that mice so caught were not injured at all.

"Or at least," he added, "not necessarily. The can or reservoir may of course be filled with water, thus drowning the little creature. But left dry it is quite safe."

He then explained the mechanism.

"You get the idea," he said. "The mouse enters here on the floor level for the cheese. As it does so it trips the door, which imprisons it quite harmlessly. After eating the cheese it naturally seeks to escape, but the door is closed. It therefore climbs this gentle winding ascent to the top of the reservoir and steps on this small plank. Its weight trips the plank and it slides painlessly into the reservoir; to life or death as you may decide."

He seemed very gratified when we purchased it, and as he was quite pleasant and even good-looking, Tish gave him a glass of cordial. This seemed to cheer him, and he stated that he was only selling mousetraps temporarily.

"I had hoped for better things," he said, with a faint smile at all of us. "I had a job. I had a future. I even had a girl. I was," he added brokenly, "very much in love with her. But in the end she failed me. Any girl who would act as she did— Well, never mind about that. Here's to the trap, ladies; and the mouse."

Before he left he said his name was Jones, and that he might drop in from time to time to see how the mechanism was operating. When I recall that, and his duplicity throughout the entire affair, I am filled with indignation. But it must be stated, here and now, that none of us were responsible for the treatment he received later during the incident at the Zoo. Or for his broken camera.

II

We spent the remainder of the afternoon in laying our plans. Tish was convinced that the family on the second floor of her apartment house would have mice, as they were most untidy. That failing, she arranged with Mr. Beilstein, her butcher, for a visit that night to his basement. And Mr. Caspari, who runs a restaurant in the neighborhood, did not keep a cat and was willing to let us into his cellar if necessary.

At last all was prepared, and we gathered together our impedimenta, consisting of the mousetrap, the package of cheese, the butterfly net, the flashlight, and the small tin of shoe blacking. With these properties, so to speak, and dressed entirely in dark garments, we felt prepared for anything, and Tish telephoned Charlie Sands and so notified him.

He seemed rather uneasy, however.

"Now see here," he protested. "You are only going after a mouse. You don't have to kill anybody. No murders, no publicity, and absolutely no trouble with the police. Is that a promise?"

To which Tish made no reply, simply hanging up the receiver. I have recorded this here, as he has since stated that we committed an absolute breach of contract. There was no contract.

Nevertheless, I must say that our first attempt that evening was most unsuccessful. Discovering that the family on the second floor was away from home, at nine o'clock that night, having blackened our faces, we went down the fire escape and entered by a window. From the disorder of the kitchen it looked most promising, and Tish was in the act of placing cheese in the trap when to our horror we heard voices in the next room.

We immediately took refuge in the kitchen closet, but here unluckily Aggie backed against a blueberry pie. It made a most frightful noise as it fell, and we barely managed to escape. And it is indicative of the way things were to go with us that night that someone put a head out of a window and screamed and that a police officer passing below saw us and followed us up the fire escape.

We had barely time to throw off our hats, wipe our faces, and dump the trap, butterfly net, cheese, flashlight, and shoe blacking into a closet when he was hammering at the window. By that time, however, Tish had sat down and picked up her knitting, and she merely glanced up.

"See what that is, Lizzie," she said calmly.

I let him in, and I must say he looked astonished

when he saw us. He took off his cap and mopped his forehead.

"Sorry, ladies," he said, "but the people on the second floor have had some burglars, and I sure thought I saw them come in here."

"Burglars?" said Tish. "What burglars? There are no burglars here, I assure you."

"I saw them clear," he said. "They had masks on."

Aggie sneezed violently, but Tish went on with her knitting.

"Dear me," she said. "Masks! I know they wear gloves, but masks! What did they take, officer?"

"They tried to take a blueberry pie," he said.

Here again Aggie sneezed and he looked at her with suspicion. But in the end Tish gave him some cordial and he became more friendly. He said his name was O'Brien; shall I ever forget it! And when he finally departed we heard him going down the fire escape and singing a song about a policeman's lot not being a happy one.

I must admit that my nerves were badly shaken, and Aggie implored us to abandon all search for a mouse that night. Tish, however, was firm.

"We have given our promise," she said, "and we are engaged in nothing nefarious. I have no intention of coming into conflict with the law."

In the end we agreed. As Mr. Beilstein's shop around the corner closed at ten o'clock, we took an immediate departure in Tish's car, placing in it the butterfly net, cheese, flashlight, mousetrap, and shoe blacking. I must say for Aggie's acumen that we had gone only a short distance when she stated that

a car was following us, and it is our misfortune
that we did not listen to her.

But we were occupied with other matters. Mr.
Beilstein was very amiable and even said that he
had already sprinkled some cheese about.

"Not that I guarantee anything," he said. "I don't
carry meat on the hoof, so to speak! But I wish you
luck, ladies."

He then said that there was a spring lock on the
front door so that we could leave when ready, and
showed us down to the cellar. It was clean but cold,
butchers not apparently requiring heat, and Aggie
started to sneeze immediately, greatly to Tish's an-
noyance.

The cellar looked exceedingly promising, and it
appeared to be a matter of only a brief time when
we would have secured our mouse and returned to
our beds.

It required but a few moments to blacken our
faces, and almost at once Tish discovered a large
hole in a corner and outlined our strategy.

"It should be quite simple," she said. "Before I
turn out the lights I shall place the trap. On hearing
any sounds Aggie will turn on the flashlight, thus
blinding the creature, and in case it escapes the trap
I shall be ready with the net."

It was thus arranged, and in a short time we were
plunged into the cold darkness. I was shivering myself, and I could hear Aggie's teeth hitting together
with a sharp clicking noise, alternating with sup-
pressed sneezes. But for a long time nothing happened. There was no pitter-patter of tiny feet, no

sounds from the trap. In due time we heard Mr.
Beilstein depart, and then to my horror Aggie moved
to me in the dark and clutched my arm.

"There's sobebody up above!" she whispered.

There was. I could hear the sounds of muffled
footsteps on the bare floor, followed by a rasp of
metal. At that instant however Tish asked for a
light, and Aggie flashed it on the hole.

There was a rat there as big as a cat, and with an
awful shriek Aggie made for the stairs. I can still
hear her voice as she hammered on the door.

"It's locked, Tish!" she shouted frantically.

"Nonsense," said Tish sternly.

"It *is* locked."

Well, Tish turned on the lights then, and the door
was locked. Never shall I forget my feelings at this
discovery or Aggie's frenzied retreat from the stairs
for fear of some murderous creature above, only
to retire there again because of the rat below, and
moaning softly. To add to our discomfort there was
the knowledge that it was Saturday night, and we
might be imprisoned until Monday morning.

The situation was most unpleasant. There were
now no sounds from above, and Tish, opening a
door, had found only a large refrigerating room,
from which came a draft of icy air.

"There is one comfort," she said thoughtfully.
"There is considerable food there, including a baked
ham. We need not starve."

"We cad freeze," said Aggie feebly. "I ab freezig
dow."

"I should think running about would keep you warm," said Tish, with disapproval.

Such was the condition of affairs that we had all forgotten about the mouse. Even Tish, while outwardly calm, must have known some anxious moments, for I recall that she brought out the ham and gave it to Aggie, who regarded it with extreme distaste. But in the end it was Tish who at last saw a narrow airshaft leading to an alley, and decided that it was a possible means of escape.

It was but the work of a moment to gather together the net, mousetrap, and other things. Then, as I am the largest of us, she urged me to make the attempt first.

By standing on a heap of coal I reached the shaft and struggled halfway through it. It seemed impossible to go farther, and I was about to retreat once more when a brilliant flash half blinded me; to my horror I felt an enormous hand on my shoulder!

"You would, would you?" said a voice. "All right, Jim. Here's one of them, and the others are inside."

It was a policeman, and there was another running to his assistance.

I do not recall a more unpleasant situation, with Aggie and our dear Tish slowly emerging from the cellar, and a police patrol appearing out of nowhere and shrieking into the alley.

Looking back, I wonder what we could have done; but how were we to know that our arrest was no accident, but part of a deliberate plot? Or that the flash which half blinded me as I stuck in the air shaft was from a camera? Or even that Aggie, dazed with terror, had brought along that wretched baked ham, and that Officer O'Brien would be at the station house where they took us, and see it?

He walked up to us and gave us a most disagreeable look.

"So!" he said. "Knitting, were you? And masks, says you! First a blueberry pie and now a ham!" He then turned to a man behind the desk and spoke to him. "Listen, sarge," he said. "They're burglars. Food burglars is what they are. What's more, they doped me. They gave me a glass of—a glass of water, and half an hour after I took it I passed out cold. Just sat down to rest my feet and was out like a light."

It was useless to explain about the blackberry cordial, although we attempted to do so, and when Tish said coldly that while unconscious he had been able to sing about a policeman's lot, he said he had never heard of it, and that maybe we needed strait-jackets. Either that, or he did.

It looked very unpleasant for all of us, especially as the mouse was a secret and we did not dare to explain. And when they brought in the trap, the cheese, the flashlight, the shoe blacking, and the butterfly net the man at the desk said we'd better be locked up until we could be put under observation.

Eventually, however, Tish prevailed on them to call up Charlie Sands. He had been asleep and was in a very bad humor. At first, what with the blacking still on our faces, he told the police captain in charge that he did not know us. Then he looked again, and closed his eyes and shuddered.

"I hate to admit it," he said, "but they're mine.
At least one of them is. And if we can go off in a
corner somewhere I guess I can explain. All but the
ham," he added firmly. "I don't propose to explain
the ham. It was not on the agenda."

It was one o'clock in the morning before we were
released, and the last thing I saw was the sergeant
at the desk with a knife, cutting at that wretched
ham while a group of hungry-looking policemen surrounded him. But on the way out Aggie caught at
my arm again and sneezed once more.

"There it is agaid," she hissed.

"What is?"

"The car that followed us," she said.

There *was* a car across the street, but when we
looked at it it moved on. Also our attention was dis-
tracted by Charlie Sands, who was looking at us
and our belongings in a most unpleasant manner.

"Now get this," he said. "The mouse business is
out. Definitely out. I don't want a mouse. I never
want to hear of a mouse again. If anyone says
'mouse' to me from now on I shall froth at the
mouth. Now I am taking you to wherever you left
your car and after that I am taking the receiver off
my telephone hook and going to bed. Is that understood?"

"You asked us to do you a favor," Tish said tartly.
"If this is your gratitude—"

"Gratitude!" he said bitterly. "Look at me! I am
aging rapidly. I am stoop-shouldered with care. If
anyone mentions the police to me I shiver, and if my

telephone rings at night I leap out of bed with a loud shriek. I ask you, why?"

He said nothing more until he had driven us back to our car. Then he saw the trap which Tish was carrying, and looked at it in surprise.

"What in God's name is that?" he demanded. "The model of a steel mill?"

"It is a mousetrap," Tish informed him.

But he merely gave a low moan, got into his car, drove off with extreme rapidity.

III

In summarizing the situation later, I can see that a number of elements contributed largely to our trouble. Certainly it is not true that we were discovered beating our unfortunate Aggie or that we inaugurated any reign of terror during the following hours; the incident of the fire hydrant was entirely accidental, and there was certainly no dog caught in the upflow of water and held there, Similarly, the situation at the peanut stand was the product of emergency.

But we have always maintained that had Charlie Sands not been incommunicado at the time of our second arrest some of these incidents need not have occurred.

For we were arrested again that night, and due to no fault of our own.

I dare say we should have gone home after that failure at the butchershop. I myself needed arnica badly, and Aggie had taken a severe cold. Tish,

however, was for going on to Caspari's, and so
as usual we followed our dauntless leader.

I must say that our entrance at the restaurant
aroused some attenion, for we had forgotten the
blacking on our faces and were still carrying the butterfly net, mousetrap, flashlight, cheese, and so on.
Indeed, I am quite certain that I saw Paula at one
of the tables, but as she at once looked away I realized
she did not know us.

Mr. Caspari was most hospitable, having even
prepared a basket of sandwiches for our long vigil,
and the moment we reached the cellar we felt that
our difficulties were over. The place was fairly over-
run with mice, and Aggie at once climbed onto a
box and, sneezing at intervals, held her skirts tightly
around her.

It was not necessary, as Tish observed, to follow
our previous technique. All that was needed was to
select a good specimen, and I shall always remember
her as, armed with the butterfly net, she stood poised
for action. Nevertheless, it was here that trouble
overtook us, and the beginning of the more serious
events of the night.

Tish had at last discovered a fine specimen on a
beam overhead and was stalking it carefully when
from the stairs there came again the same blinding
flash of light as had followed our arrest; and this
was followed by a series of bloodcurdling screams
from Aggie.

In an instant she had leaped from the box and, in
spite of our efforts to calm her, ran still shrieking
up the stairs and into the restaurant. By the time

Tish and I had picked up our impedimenta she had reached the street and was in fact almost a block away.

Encumbered as we were it was some time before we reached her, and then only because she had virtually collapsed onto a doorstep. She was so exhausted that we had to bend over her to hear her.

"What in the world happened to you?" Tish demanded.

It was with an effort that Aggie spoke.

"The bouse," she whispered. "You docked it idside my waist. It's there dow."

She then broke into loud weeping, and it was while we were exploring for the creature that the police car drew up and two men jumped out and jerked us away with terrific force.

"Shame on you," said one of them. "Attacking a defenseless woman! What did you lose, lady? A pocketbook?"

Aggie pulled herself together and suddenly clapped her hand to her mouth.

"By upper teeth," she said wildly. "I've lost by upper teeth."

They seemed astounded, for one of them observed that that was a new one to him.

"Now see here," he said to Tish. "You give this poor soul her teeth, and then we'll go to the station house and put you two dentists where you can work on each other."

It was in vain that we attempted to explain, and Aggie was of little assistance. True, the mouse had

either gone or was quiescent, but her mind was entirely occupied with her missing teeth. In a sort of
dreadful silence we were taken once more to the
police station, only to find that Officer O'Brien was
still there and that he grinned most disagreeably
when he heard the charge.

"Teeth!" he said. "My God, they not only steal
food. They steal the teeth to chew it with!"

We were greatly relieved when a police matron,
having searched Aggie, found no mouse; and as her
teeth were certainly not in our possession, and she
would make no charge of assault against us, we
were finally released. Just before we departed, however, Officer O'Brien lifted the lid of Mr. Caspari's
basket and saw the sandwiches, and I thought his
eyes would pop out of his head.

"Now listen, sarge," he said earnestly. "I can
swallow the butterfly net if you say so. I'll swallow
the mousetrap, and even the mouse, if you say the
word. But either there's something screwy about
these women gathering up food or I'm a two-headed
tapeworm."

He was still staring at us as we departed, and I
remember that he followed us into the street, observing that the next time he could do with a stein of
beer and some pretzels. But we ignored him and the
last we saw of him for some hours was as he stood
on the pavement, mopping his forehead with his
handkerchief and gazing after us.

It required some time to recover the teeth, but
we found them at last, fortunately unbroken. And

it was at that moment that Aggie, glancing up from the search, caught at my arm and said that the mysterious car had followed us once more.

This time there was no doubt of it. It was coming slowly along, and when it reached us it stopped.

What was our relief when a familiar figure emerged, and a familiar voice spoke to us.

"Well, ladies," it said. "What luck so far?"

It was Mr. Smith.

I pause here to recall that moment, and to justify our further conduct. What reason had we to suspect him, especially as he at once stated that he had followed us throughout the evening for our own protection, and that he knew the purpose of our search.

"And what is that purpose?" Tish demanded sharply.

He looked up and down the street before he replied.

"The code word is 'mouse,'" he said, "and I am here to help if possible. So far I gather that you have been unfortunate, but I hope you will not abandon the project."

Why should we have suspected him? He stood there, tall and smiling, and said that the night was still young and mice were not really active until the entire city slept. Even church mice, he added, because they have nothing really to get up for.

I must say that none of us was at all eager to go on. Aggie indeed was insistent on going home, and even our dear Tish was uncertain. He looked much disappointed, and drew a long breath.

"It would be a pity," he said, "with everything depending on you. I hate to be a quitter. Also I have given my word to—to one of the girls at the office, and I hate to let her down. Not that she cares what I do," he added despondently, "but after all—"

Tish is always interested in love affairs, and so she drew the story from him. He had, he said, been engaged to this young woman, but a small incident had separated them. He said also that he would always respect her, but that there was no use going home to bed because all he did was lie awake and think about her. What he really thought he would do if we abandoned the search would be to catch up in his drinking, because in that way he could forget her, and anyhow while engaged to her he had been on the wagon.

Nor was the offer of coffee as a substitute for strong drink of any avail.

"Coffee only keeps me awake," he said dejectedly. "I lie awake and think about her eyes and her smile, and the way she acted when—well, never mind about that. I'll show her. That's all."

"Not on liquor," said Tish firmly.

But he did not listen. Instead, he prepared to leave us.

"I'm sorry," he said. "Sorry you've quit on the thing. The boys and girls at the office will be sorry too. Well, that's life. I was going to suggest the Zoo, but what's the use? Good night."

It was obviously impossible to let him leave us in that frame of mind, and our dear Tish perceived this immediately. It was for this reason, and this reason alone, that she detained him.

"What about the Zoo?" she inquired.

"Nothing much. Lots of mice there, that's all. Mouse heaven, that's what it is. Now you take Babe, the elephant. She likes mice. Gentle as a kitten, Babe is. Lets them play around her all night. But never mind about that. I'll tell the folks you tried anyhow."

He was about to drive away when Tish called to him, and I recognized her old militant voice once more.

"If you will take us to our car at Caspari's," she said, "we will follow you to the Zoo."

It will be seen from this how simple—indeed inevitable—was the series of events which led to the final one. Who among us could have guessed at Mr. Jones's duplicity? Or, to give him his due, could have known that in the hour of our need he would be helpless? Would indeed suffer actual physical indignity and such a black eye as I have seldom seen?

Or who would have suspected that, in spite of the search, our poor Aggie was still harboring the mouse, and that very probably within one of the pads which—being flat of chest—she wears inside her dress?

My reply to all of that is—nobody.

IV

The Zoo was close at hand, and for two or three blocks we followed Mr. Jones's car without difficulty. Tish was driving with Aggie beside her, while in the rear I was in charge of the butterfly net, mousetrap, cheese, and flashlight. No one was more amazed

than I, therefore, when suddenly Aggie gave a most
terrific shriek and rose up in her seat.

"It's movig," she said. "I felt it."

"Of course, it's moving," said Tish calmly.
"What's a car for? Sit down and don't be an idiot."

Aggie merely screamed again and tried to leap out
of the car; in the attempt to hold her we narrowly
missed a police officer and struck a fire plug. Almost
immediately we were in the center of a water spout,
and the policeman was picking himself up from the
pavement and coming toward us with a most terrible
look on his face.

It was Officer O'Brien!

It was a dreadful moment, for he had recognized
us at once and was splashing toward us while using
the most shocking language. As it was obvious that
he intended to arrest us, and as he was even threatening bodily attack, I am quite certain that Tish took
the only course possible.

She reached back for the butterfly net and as he
caught at the door brought it down firmly over his
head.

There was no other violence, in spite of his statement later as to a broken nose. Nor was he justified
in shooting at our tires as we drove off. As to the
dog, none of us saw one at the fire plug, and certainly it was not injured.

Mr. Jones, some distance ahead, had known nothing of this incident, and as we were moving rapidly
it was not until we had almost reached the Zoo that
Tish stopped the car and confronted Aggie.

"Now," she said. "What was moving?"

"The bouse," said Aggie feebly.

"What mouse? Don't be absurd. You have no mouse."

"It was id by bosob," said Aggie and burst into tears.

However, as it now appeared to be gone, or at least quiescent, Tish drove on again.

We were still very wet when we reached the park which houses the Zoo, and Mr. Jones looked slightly surprised when we found him. When we explained he simply nodded.

"I see," he said. "Only a fire hydrant. I thought maybe you'd broken open the reservoir. And you put the butterfly net on a policeman? Well, I've always wanted to see a butterfly net on a policeman, but again—well, that's life, isn't it?"

He remained thoughtful for a moment or so, merely observing that he was glad we had not started out to catch a hippopotamus. Then he explained his plan to us.

"I can get in myself," he said. "I used to write stories of the place at night. In the days," he added bitterly, "when I thought I could write. But you ladies will have to get in by stealth, so to speak. And if you see a watchman," he went on, "it will not be necessary to kill him. He may have a family. Just lie low and let him pass."

I must say that it seemed simple enough. He was to gain admittance on a card or something he had, while we were to climb the fence into the enclosure where Babe took the air on pleasant days, and there unbolt the sliding door from the outside. Then when the chance came he would get into her pen or cage or whatever it is and so admit us. Aggie looked rather pale at this, but he again observed that Babe was the pet of the Zoo; if she stuck out her trunk, we had only to pet it gently and pass on.

It did seem queer to us that he then produced a camera from his car, but he explained it quite easily.

"Our photographer is sick," he said, "and they have a new elephant here somewhere. He asked me to get a flashlight picture for him if I could."

He showed us where to go and then disappeared, but I must confess that any enthusiasm I may have felt as to a mouse for Charlie Sands had entirely vanished. Even Tish, usually so high-spirited, was silent, and Aggie was actually trembling.

"I wish I'd brought sobe peaduts," she said to me in a low voice. "I'd feel safer."

Encumbered as we still were with the trap, the flashlight, the cheese, the fence proved rather difficult. Luckily for us, the heavy steel posts were reinforced with a metal netting, and with this as a foothold we finally managed it. Nevertheless, as the minutes went on and a cold wind arose, our dampened condition made us most uncomfortable. Reference to Tish's watch showed us that the hour by then was 3:00 A.M., but the Zoo was not entirely quiet. Every now and then some creature or other gave a piercing scream, and something else either barked or howled. Nor were matters improved by the passage at that time of a night watchman. At Tish's whispered suggestion we lay down on the cement, and he did not see us. Nevertheless, we were greatly relieved when at last we heard a low voice beyond the door.

"Quiet, Babe," it said. "It's all right. It's only me."

It was Mr. Jones, and immediately after he slid open the door a bit and squeezed through. It seemed to me that he came through rather rapidly, and that a dull thud shook the door as he left it; but in a moment he was his usual nonchalant self, although somewhat breathless.

"I wakened her rather suddenly," he explained. "Better give her a minute or two to recover. I'm like that myself," he said, smiling. "Rouse me too quickly and I—well, I don't like it."

He added that he had seen several mice in the cage—which actually was a large room and not a cage at all—and that all we had to do was to enter quietly and let Babe get used to us by standing still for a brief time. After that, he said, we could all go about our business, as she was chained by one foot and would probably go back to sleep again anyhow.

With that he shoved the door back a foot or two, and we squeezed inside, Tish as usual leading the way, and Mr. Jones closing the door behind us.

The cage was dim, the only light being through the bars from somewhere beyond, but even at that it seemed to me that Babe had grown somewhat since last I saw her. I had little time for these observations, however, as at that moment she whipped out her trunk and jerked my hat from my head. Mr. Jones looked rather surprised and somewhat apologetic.

"Hope you don't mind," he said. "She's a playful old girl. Like a kitten, aren't you, Babe? Come on now. Be a sport. Give it up, Babe."

But Babe had put her foot on it and was already tearing it to pieces; when he tried to stoop and recover it, she gave a squeal and made a pass at him with her trunk. I must say he looked uncomfortable.

"I don't know, ladies," he said in a worried voice. "She doesn't seem to be in the mood, does she? If you'd care to try somewhere else—"

"Id the liod's cage, I suppose," said Aggie coldly.

Tish refused to go elsewhere. Whether Babe was in the mood or not, there were certainly mice there, and lacking now the net, she was busily baiting the trap with the cheese and placing it in a corner. In the end Mr. Jones left us there, going to get his camera, which he had hidden somewhere, as they had a new keeper who didn't like the animals disturbed at night.

Before he left he warned us.

"If anybody comes along," he said, "just flatten yourselves against the wall and keep quiet."

Babe made another pass at him with her trunk as he went out, and I saw him stop and hesitate outside. Then he went on, and we were alone. Alone that is save for the elephant, who had now finished my hat and was squealing and still apparently nervous. But Tish was not anxious. Already a mouse had entered the lower portion of the trap, and as she said, it was only a matter of time until, finding itself closed in, it would climb to the top, trip the plank and drop into the reservoir.

But Aggie in the meantime had discovered something, and was staring at me with a pale face.

"Lizzie!" she said. "Isn't Babe a lady?"

I had no time whatever to reply. There was the blinding light of Mr. Jones's flash, and then a man's voice shouting angrily.

"Here, stop that!" he yelled. "What the hell do you mean?"

This was immediately followed by the sounds of two men in a struggle and a loud startled trumpeting by Babe. I fancied, too, that I heard a faint squeal from Aggie and that Tish in a low voice was telling us to keep still. But my eyes were on the passage beyond the bars where Mr. Jones, looking slightly dazed, was being marched off by an irate keeper who was apparently also kicking the camera in front of him.

When I turned, what a sight met my eyes! Our poor Aggie was completely encircled by the elephant's trunk and was being held high in the air. What is more, a door had clanged shut in the distance and we were now alone in our dreadful situation.

It was as usual Tish who recovered first, and her immediate thought was for our unfortunate companion.

"Are you all right, Aggie?" she asked anxiously.

What a comfort to hear her voice in reply, feeble as it was.

"Do," she said.

I draw a veil over what followed: our vain attempts to coax Babe to let her down, or even to allow

us to approach her; the roars and trumpetings all
through the building, so that our calls for help were
unheard; even my own frantic excursion into the
passage, lined with cages on both sides, to find that
we were securely locked in; and my return to find
that Babe had placed Aggie on the top of her head
and was swinging her trunk to keep us at a distance.

It was indeed a most unhappy experience, and it
was Tish who brought her practical mind to the
problem.

"It is evident," she said, "that we must placate her
in some way. I am sorry to blame anybody, but Mr.
Jones's use of the flash for a photograph has upset
her badly. If we had some peanuts, for instance—"

"Peaduts!" said Aggie in a dreadful voice. "Get
a gud ad kill her."

Here she sneezed violently, and the elephant
swung its trunk up again and trumpeted in a most
threatening manner.

As I have said, it is easy now to see the simple and
yet inevitable sequence of events. What could Tish
do but what she did do? And this at the very moment of her triumph, with the mouse in the trap and
practically ours. It was for this and no other reason
that she broke into the peanut stand near by and was
arrested while so doing. She had already placed the
money for the broken glass on the counter, and also
for the half dozen packages of peanuts in her possession, when the park policeman discovered her.

It is unfortunate that he refused to listen to her
explanation, and should be a lesson to the police in
general. For she had carried the mousetrap with

her, and when she tried to explain it, and that Aggie
was in the clutches of the elephant, he simply did not
believe her.

"All right," he said. "All right. Just take it easy,
sister. You can tell that to the doctors."

"To what doctors?"

"Where you're going," he said, and telephoned
for an ambulance.

It was in vain that she protested. She was obliged
to stand by, securely held, while he telephoned that
he had caught a woman in the Zoo who was stealing
peanuts to feed to a mouse to feed to the elephant.
What is more, he took the trap from her and threw
it away!

By that time she was desperate, and I believe that
he had to call for help. It seems unfortunate that it
was Officer O'Brien who first arrived, and that he
was about to manacle her brutally when he saw the
peanuts and stood back.

"My Gawd!" he said, almost with reverence.
"What an appetite!"

He soon recovered and stated that she had tried
twice that night to kill him, and that his nose was
broken and would never be the same again. In the
end I believe it required three men to get her into
the ambulance, thence to be taken to the psychopathic
ward of the hospital and tied to a bed. As I have
said, she had been on the board there for many years,
but no one recognized her; and when she spoke of
Aggie's dire situation they merely gave her a seda-
tive. . . .

Needless to say, neither Aggie nor I knew anything of this at the time. We were occupied with our own problem, and I for one cannot put on paper my sentiments as the time passed and Tish did not return. The elephant showed no signs of relenting, and the sight of Aggie's desperate face high above was more than I could bear.

In the end I decided to follow Tish and see what had happened, although Aggie protested wildly.

"Don't be foolish," I told her. "Mr. Jones said she was playful. She's playing now. That's all it is."

"Just good clead fud!" said Aggie. "Well, let her play with you for a while. I'be fed up. I'd rather have a bouse, ady bidute."

Here she sneezed once more, and the elephant simply coiled its trunk around her and raised her into the air. I waited only long enough to see her safe on its head again and then hastened outside to the fence. I needed help, and most of all I needed Tish. Behind me I could hear Aggie's plaintive calls, but I dared not stop. However, misfortune pursued us all that dreadful night; for I had climbed the fence with some difficulty and had just reached the ground when a man caught hold of me, and I recognized the watchman we had seen before. Never have I felt such relief, and never have I been so shocked as when he shook me violently.

"So that's the game, is it?" he said. "I'll teach the lot of you. By God, if you reporters won't even let the animals sleep—!"

"Listen," I said in a frantic voice. "I'm not a reporter. We came to catch a mouse, that's all. A live mouse. And Aggie—"

"What did you want a mouse for?" he asked, staring at me.

"To stuff," I said. "To hang on a wall. To—"

It is incredible, but after that he would not even listen to me! I told him about Aggie, and my fears for Tish, but he only held on to me and shook his head.

"You just come with me, nice and quiet," he said. "You come along and we'll find a mouse for you; a nice quiet mouse to hang on the wall."

He took me into an office somewhere, and all the night people at the Zoo came and looked at me. They even pretended to believe my story, but I could see that they did not, and when in a frenzy I tried to escape and get back to Aggie they locked me in.

V

It was broad daylight when Mr. Jones, with a quite dreadful black eye, came to release me; and it was much later before the entire staff of the Zoo managed to rescue our poor Aggie. And it was then that I learned the truth, that Babe was not Babe at all, but the new elephant, and that it had taken a fancy to Aggie and was most unwilling to let her go.

Our reunion in that office of the Zoo was touching, and it was not long before we reached Tish's apartment. It is easy to imagine our horror when we found that she was not there. Instead, a red-eyed Hannah said that Charlie Sands was out searching for her, and there was only Paula, gazing out the window and rather drooping.

She brightened when she saw us, but stiffened when she caught sight of Mr. Jones, and gave him a dreadful look.

"Well!" she said. "And where do *you* come in on this?"

"I've been in on it all night. And if you think it's been easy, look at me."

"I am looking," she said nastily. "The only thing I see to admire is that eye."

"If that's the way you feel—"

"That's exactly the way I feel, Bill Lawrence," she said coldly.

Then at last we knew the truth, and the shocking deception that had been practiced on us. But he did not appear at all ashamed. He merely gave Paula a long look.

"All right," he said. "All right. Since that's your state of mind, I know where I can go. And get a job too. A jail's a darned good place to write, and during the small hours of this morning I did a bit of work. However—"

He then prepared to depart, but she leaped at him and caught his arm.

"Write what?" she demanded.

He pulled some yellow paper from his pocket and glanced at it.

"It's called 'The Mouse,'" he said, "and maybe the *Gazette* won't eat it up, photographs and all! It begins as follows—"

She snatched at the paper, but he held it away from her.

"Bill!" she said. "You wouldn't! You wouldn't

spoil everything. You wouldn't let me down like this, would you?"

"Wouldn't I?" he said, with a bitter laugh. "Lister, my girl. You thought it was damned funny when that moose got me in a tree, didn't you? It was a laugh, wasn't it? It was a good laugh when I lost my job too."

"Bill, I never laughed at that."

"Didn't you?" he said coldly. "Well, laugh this off. I've got the story of my life here. To get it I have committed felonious entry, barratry and mayhem, been chased by a new elephant at the Zoo, hit by a fellow with a fist like a ham, and spent two hours in a jail cell. I'm not selling."

Well, I must say I was surprised at her: instead of being angry, she went to him and stroked the sleeve of his coat, looking up at him with a little smile.

"If you're not selling, Bill, maybe you're trading," she said. "I'm sorry, Bill. I've missed you."

To our amazement he grabbed her and shook her violently. Then he simply put his arms around her and kissed the top of her head.

"Of course I'm trading, darling," he said. "What the devil do you think I did it for?"

I must say they seemed entirely to have forgotten us until Aggie sneezed. They looked a bit sheepish then, but when I told them we had no mouse Paula looked rather vague.

"Mouse?" she said. "Oh, yes, I'd forgotten. Well, it doesn't really matter. We can get one somewhere."

Aggie went at once to bed, the hay in the elephant

cage having greatly increased her hay fever; but I remained on watch in a frenzy of anxiety. The thought of our dear Tish alone somewhere and in trouble was more than I could bear; and when the telephone rang I rushed to it.

It was only Mr. Beilstein to inquire how the night had gone. When he heard my voice he said, "And did you get a nice liddle mouse, Miss Lizzie?"

"We got an elephant," I said tartly.

"An elephant? In my cellar?"

But I hung up. I felt that I could bear no more. . . .

It was fully noon before Charlie Sands located Tish. She was in a room at the local hospital in the psycopathic ward, and as I have said, tied to the bed. The doctor in charge took him in and observed that it was a very sad case.

"You take women of a certain age," he said, "and you often get a psychosis of this nature. Man becomes the animal in pursuit, in this case an elephant, and—"

Charlie Sands pushed him aside and confronted Tish, who merely closed her eyes.

"What does this mean?" was his opening speech, in a stern voice. "Open your eyes and look at me. *What* about an elephant?"

"Aggie's on it," she said. "I've told them that but they won't believe me."

"You see," said the doctor. "She's been saying that ever since she was brought here. Trying to escape too, so she had to be restrained."

But Charlie Sands was not listening. He got a chair and sat down by the bed, and I believe he asked for a glass of water.

"All right," he said. "Aggie's on an elephant somewhere, but you're here. Why? And how?"

"I was merely trying to get some peanuts. That's all."

"What for?"

And then Tish became her old self.

"Don't be a fool," she said sharply. "For the elephant, of course."

He looked so strange that a nurse brought him some aromatic ammonia. He waved it away, however, as Tish spoke again.

"I had just captured a good mouse," she said, "but the policeman threw it away."

"A mouse!" said the doctor. "Now that's new. She has mentioned a fire hydrant—symbolic, of course—and, curiously enough, a baked ham. But a mouse—that's strange."

"You don't know her," said Charlie Sands bitterly. "It's not strange. It's quite normal. Ask her for a steel rivet and she'd go after the Brooklyn Bridge." He then stood up and gazed down at Tish. "I have a theory," he said, "that if I could leave you here life would be a long, sweet song. Dull perhaps, but quiet. However—" He drew a long breath. "You'd better tell me where this elephant is. Aggie may be tired of it." . . .

It was some hours later that our dear Tish returned home, and it was only after Charlie Sands had had a glass or two of our blackberry cordial that he at last heard the full story of the night.

"I see," he said finally. "Of course, it is all quite easy, once you understand. Merely theft, assault and battery, destruction of property, attacking a policeman, and so on." He then poured himself another glass of the cordial and finally grinned.

"It must have been quite a night for Bill," he said. "Well, he's a stronger man than I am."

He seemed relieved when he heard that Paula had got the story and burned it. But he shook his head.

"That's love," he said, "and heaven defend me from it."

It was then that Hannah came in, holding a Mason jar, and there was a live mouse in it! She had found it in the pantry that morning.

I believe that they had the head mounted later on, and that Bill Lawrence, who had been reinstated, made the presentation speech. I believe also that the old man, as they call the managing editor, took the hint and even smiled, and that the mouse hangs in his office today. But only yesterday Tish, coming home from the market, dropped her basket and food of all sorts rolled over the pavement.

She was picking up what she could when Officer O'Brien came by. He stopped and gave her a hard look.

"I see you've had a good day," he said, and walked on.

TISH
GOES TO JAIL

TISH GOES TO JAIL

I

ONLY THE other day, while our poor Aggie was still recovering from the shock of our recent night high above the city, I read the story of a man somewhere in the country who passed a red lantern and, running plump into a circus which was on the move, actually ended with an enormous and indignant elephant sitting on the radiator of his car. As our introduction to the terrible affair which landed both Tish Carberry and me in jail bears some resemblance to this incident, I at once determined to make a record of what actually occurred.

To know all is to forgive all, and I must say that the press has been very unkind, especially to Tish. She was actuated throughout only by the highest principles, and even while stoically sitting in that dreadful cell she was calm and self-contained.

"I don't even know what you are talking about," she said to Charlie Sands. "If I have tried to help a pair of young lovers, that is entirely my affair. I have committed no felony."

"Maybe not in this state," he said coldly, "but in some parts of this great and glorious Union shooting at a sheriff and then filling him full of splinters is not regarded with any favor."

"He slipped," said Tish calmly.

"He says you pushed him," Charlie Sands retorted. "I've been in to see him, and he has two constables and a deputy working over him with tweezers."

He then looked at me and accused me of shooting a state trooper—which, as everyone now knows, was purely accidental, the man being out of the hospital the next day. And only then did he notice Aggie's absence and demand to know where she was.

"So far as I know," said Tish with her usual dignity, "she is still in the top of the tree."

"The tree?" he said, looking astonished. "What tree? What do you mean, a tree?"

"A tree in the mountains," Tish explained patiently. "We had to leave her there."

I must say he looked bewildered at that.

"I see," he said. "You left her in a tree. But what was she doing in a tree? Building a nest?"

We explained then, but when he finally left us it was with a strange look on his face; and we heard later that he sat down somewhere outside for a lengthy period, appearing rather dazed.

However, that is the end of the story, and I must relate the events which led up to it.

It was early autumn when both Aggie and I noticed that Tish was growing restless, and one day while we were there the evening paper came, and she merely crumpled it into a ball and threw it into the wastebasket.

"I am not a nervous woman," she said, "but when

all the news I read is bad it is time to call a halt. Not only is crime rampant in the land, but there is even a possibility that the Communists will drive us into a state of revolution. In that case, where will we be?"

"I know where I will be," I said firmly. "I'll be in the front row of the mob, waving the red flag and singing Russian songs with the best of them. If you think I'm going to lay my head on any guillotine, you can think again."

I am afraid that this displeased her, for she was silent for some time; and when at last she spoke, it was to say that there was but one refuge from both revolution and crime, and that was some quiet spot in the country.

"What we need," she said, "is a small farm, capable of supporting us all in case of necessity, and in the interval providing peace and contentment. A subsistence homestead, to use the words of our present Administration. That is all I ask during these turbulent days subsistence and to be at peace."

Aggie at once protested, as a ragweed even ten miles away greatly aggravates her hay fever; but Tish was firm, and some weeks later she notified us that she had bought a small farm.

"It lies," she said, "at the foot of heavily wooded mountains, which will offer us sanctuary if necessary. And as it is only thirty miles from here it is easy of access. I shall hope to spend my declining days there in contemplation and quiet."

Well, that—as Charlie Sands observed—was something. We did not, however, see the place that winter, as it had no heating plant, and the only news we had about it was when Charlie Sands went there once to shoot pheasants that fall.

I must say that he was rather vague about it when he returned.

"It's all right for them as likes it," he said.

What is important is that he said he had left his shotgun there, a fact which the newspapers used later to reveal us in the darkest possible colors; as a matter of record, the only time the wretched thing was fired by any of us, I did it by accident, and it knocked out a perfectly good pivot tooth, which I almost swallowed.

Late in the winter, however, Tish began to think of the farm with a certain yearning. The crime wave had broken out again, and Mr. Ostermaier, our clergyman, returned from the parish house one night to find that his best cuff links and a ten-dollar bill hidden in the toe of a shoe had been taken. Also a sensational paper reported that the daughter of one of our wealthy citizens, a girl named Edith Lee, had been threatened with kidnaping for ransom and was under police protection.

We did not know her, but Tish was moved to profound indignation. I remember that Charlie Sands was dining with her that night, as were Aggie and myself, and she expressed herself strongly. Charlie Sands, however, was more calm.

"I imagine she can take care of herself," he observed. "There is a story that she was kidnaped a year or two ago, and that two strong men with tears in their eyes brought her back the next day and left her on the doorstep."

That was all that occurred at the dinner and, so far as I recall it, was the only mention of the girl ever made in my hearing. Charlie Sands left soon after and, having had one or two glasses of our blackberry cordial, declared that with a propeller and a gallon of oil he could swim the Atlantic Ocean. And shortly after he had gone came the incident of the bat.

I relate it here only because of the unpleasant emphasis placed later on the bottle of chloroform found by the police in Tish's bathroom, and partly used. To say that it was used for any nefarious purpose is manifestly absurd.

He had been gone only a short time when we heard a curious flapping against the walls and ceiling; and Aggie, who had worn her new switch that night, suddenly caught a sofa pillow and held it on top of her head.

"It's a bat!" she cried wildly. "Open the windows, somebody! Help! Help!"

Tish managed to silence her, but as the creature was now making various low dives, we tied towels over our heads and attempted to drive it outside. It would go no farther than the curtain, however, where it hung upside down and stared at us with a truly hideous expression.

It was all most unpleasant, especially as Hannah had gone and we were alone with it. Tish's active mind, however, was at work; and as the bat remained in the same position for some time, she turned to me.

"Get the vacuum cleaner from the closet, Lizzie," she said, "and take the thing off the end of the tube. We shall then be able to capture the creature without cruelty."

"And thed what?" said Aggie, with whom excitement always affects the nasal passages.

"We can consider that when the time comes," Tish replied calmly.

Well, I brought the cleaner and, although the creature seemed suspicious when it began to operate, it allowed us to bring the end fairly close to it. In a short time the suction caught it; it was too large to go through the tube, but was held as securely as a butterfly impaled on a pin. It was certainly an ugly thing, and Tish surveyed it with distaste.

"We can release it," she said thoughtfully, "or we can put it to a painless death."

"Drowd it," said Aggie in a bloodthirsty voice. "Drowdig is painless."

Tish, however, had a better idea, and at once requested me to get some chloroform from the drugstore. This I did, and soon the bat lay still and quite dead on the floor. If anyone still doubts this story, it is only necessary to consult the pharmacist himself. And I myself put the chloroform bottle back in Tish's closet, where, as the result of a single humane act, it was to be used so shockingly against her.

Aggie's cries for help, however, had been heard, plus the smashing of one or two vases during the excitement; and as the janitor later circulated the rumor that we had actually had a battle in the apartment there was a distinct coldness to all of us among the neighbors.

It was for this reason that we went to the farm early the following spring. Also, the crime wave still continued. There was a rumor that the Lee family had been sent another threat and that the girl was in hiding somewhere; and one rainy night Aggie came in breathless from prayer meeting, to say that a man had followed her and tried to take her umbrella. When she screamed, he pretended that he had been merely following what he had thought was one of the young girls from the choir, but it was evident that no one was now safe, and Tish finally determined to seek sanctuary in the country.

II

Before we moved out we made a preliminary visit to the farm, and both Aggie and I were most favorably impressed. It had certain deficiencies, as I have noted, but it lay on a slope, with wooded mountains behind it, and below in the valley were the summer estates of several wealthy families.

Nevertheless, that night was to see the real beginning of our troubles. It was a calm and quiet evening, and we had no premonition whatever as, through the darkness, we drove in Tish's car down the hill and onto the main road. I remember that Tish was commenting on the simplicity and honesty of the rural districts.

"The very air," she said, "smells of peace. Who could imagine violence here, or trickery?"

And then it happened. We had just passed the driveway into one of the summer estates, when suddenly and without warning a man stepped into the road and waved a red lantern.

We had been moving rapidly, and as Tish suddenly applied the brakes I was thrown forward against the windshield with considerable force. When I recovered, Aggie was picking herself off the floor of the car, and as the man approached us she gave a wild shriek.

"He's a bandit, Tish!" she gasped. "He's got a gun!"

We could now observe him distinctly, and a more dreadful figure I have never seen. He wore a handkerchief tied over his face, and as he came striding toward us he looked enormous in that light. But his first words surprised us.

"You little fool!" he said. "Did you think you'd got away with it?"

Tish had recovered her speech by that time, and she answered him indignantly.

"I object to your language," she said coldly. "As to getting away with anything— Give him my purse, Lizzie. It has two dollars and sixty-five cents in it. If that is the value he places on his immortal soul—"

To my surprise, however, he did not take the purse. Instead, he merely lifted the lantern and inspected us, and then, to our horror, he began to laugh. It took him some time to stop, and when he spoke it was in a choked voice.

"My apologies, ladies," he said. "You see, I

thought— But never mind what I thought. Just drive
on and forget it."

"And leave you to attack other innocent women?"
Tish demanded.

"Oh, come, come," he said. "I haven't attacked
you, have I? You've still got your two dollars and
sixty-five cents. You've still got your—er—honor."
Here he paused and inspected the car, which is far
from new. "You've still got your automobile too.
That's fair enough, isn't it?"

Tish, however, was not satisfied. He had quite a
cultivated voice, and was evidently far above the
usual gangster in type.

"Something quite dreadful must have driven you
to the highway," she said. "Surely you have people,
a family, perhaps even a mother. What would she
say, could she see you now?"

This seemed to touch him, for he was silent for a
moment.

Then he said:

"I am sorry, ladies, but I cannot discuss such sub-
jects. They are too sacred. When I think of my
home—" He seemed suddenly overcome with emo-
tion. "Drive on and forget me," he said huskily. "If
anyone had told me six months ago that I would be
standing in this road with a gun in my hand— But
enough of that," he said, his voice growing hard.
"Tell me," he went on, "have any of you seen a car
something like this tonight, containing a redheaded
girl who looks like a forest fire and has a disposition
like a wildcat?"

We had not, and said so. Whereupon he gave what sounded like a groan, and seemed to take a tighter grip on his revolver.

"It's as well," he said ominously. "It's as well, and then some. Because if I ever lay my hands on that imp of Satan I shall make her stand for a week."

"Stand!" Aggie repeated.

"Stand," he said firmly. "She'll stand because she won't want to sit. I'm fed up. I'm fed up so full that I'm practically gorged. If she comes here tonight, she'll be sorry. That's all."

We all felt most uneasy, and Tish inquired if he would dare to mistreat a young and innocent girl in that manner. At this, however, he gave a hollow laugh.

"Young and innocent!" he said bitterly. "Listen to me. She may be young, all right, but she's been raising hell ever since she wore diapers. If she thinks she can get away with this, she's mistaken her man. That's all." But he saw our faces at that moment, and added: "Don't worry; I shan't kill her. That would be too easy! All right, ladies. Just move along and forget you saw me."

He then stepped back into the bushes, and Tish started the car again. Aggie was sneezing with excitement, and I must say that even Tish seemed slightly upset. In fact, we had gone only half a mile or so when she suddenly stopped the car.

"We must go back," she said in a determined voice. "He dislikes that girl intensely, and I don't believe he is a bandit. He is probably a discarded lover, and as such is dangerous. We must not leave her to her fate, whatever it may be."

I remember begging her not to do anything so rash, and Aggie flatly refused to leave the car. However, anyone who knows Tish Carberry and her hatred of wrong and injustice will know that nothing moved her. She was already on her way, and as I was unwilling to leave her to her fate I followed her. The last sound I heard was our poor Aggie sneezing in the car.

It was indeed a strange journey, for soon Tish left the road and took to the fields. In the darkness it was quite impossible to see, and at least twice I was caught in barbed wire, and once I stepped into a mud hole and lost a shoe, with no chance of retrieving it.

At last, however, we were behind the embankment where we had been held up, and could plainly see the bandit, or whatever he was, lurking beside the road. He had dropped the mask and was smoking a cigarette, but he was evidently still in a bad humor, for once he lighted a match and looked at his watch, and we could hear him swearing in a most unseemly manner.

We waited there for two hours.

It was certainly a dreadful time. I was cramped, the air was cold, and to add to our anxiety, every now and then a car would come along and he would flag it. But nothing really occurred until midnight, when a car came along very swiftly, and he seemed to know it at once.

I felt Tish brace herself beside me as he waved the lantern, and my heart sank as the car stopped.

"What's the matter?" called a clear girlish voice.

"Get out of that car," he said in a most surly manner. "What the hell do you mean by stealing it and running away? Get out, I tell you!"

And then followed a most surprising situation, for the girl merely sat still.

"Oh, for crying out loud!" she said in a tired voice. "It's you again, is it? Get out of my way or I'll run over you."

She actually started the engine, and with a furious step he was beside her. In the excitement the handkerchief fell off his face, but he did not seem to notice it.

"Listen," he said; "you're a pestiferous little idiot, and for two cents I'd yank you out of that car and shake some sense into you. Where have you been?"

"That's my business," she said angrily. "And if you think I'm afraid of you, you can think again. You and your wooden gun!"

In a second she had stepped on the gas and the car was moving. That, however, was apparently more than he could bear, for at once two shots rang out and the car ran straight into the ditch and stopped.

It was so horrible that I could not even scream, and indeed it was some days later before we knew that one of the bullets had gone through Tish's hat from front to back.

As it was, there was a dreadful silence, and we expected to find the poor child slumped in her seat. But to our surprise she began to crawl out of the car.

"You would think of that," she said bitterly. "And they're your tires. Don't ask me to pay for them."

"All right," he said. "You asked for it and you got it. Now you can walk home and like it."

Well, I must say we were puzzled; especially as all he did after that was to turn off the road and disappear, leaving her standing there. When Tish and I reached her, however, she seemed quite composed. She got out a cigarette and lit it, and then coolly looked us over.

"Sorry to disappoint you," she said, "but there is no corpse. That was just a friend of mine. He gets steamed up like that now and then."

"Then he is a danger to the community and should be locked up," said Tish grimly.

For some reason that seemed to amuse her; but after a moment she looked toward the car in the ditch and scowled.

"I'll get him for that," she said in an ominous tone. "He may think he has his troubles, but he hasn't started yet."

With that she left us abruptly, and the last we saw the car was still in the ditch and she was walking up the road, alone.

All in all, it was most bewildering, and Tish spoke only once.

"It may be," she said, "that this is the love-making of a strange and new generation. I believe they have changed greatly from my mother's day. But if it is not—"

That was indeed a portentous and most unhappy night, for, on reaching the car, our dear Aggie was not in it, and a peculiar and overwhelming odor pervaded the entire atmosphere. It was not for some time that we located her among some bushes, and then she stated that a kitten had jumped into the car and she had petted it, with dire results.

We had some difficulty in getting her out of her retreat, for she had abandoned most of her clothing; but at last we did so, and it was on our way into town, with Aggie clad largely in a motor rug, that I voiced my first uncertainty as to the country as a place of residence.

"I can stand a great deal, Tish," I said, "but I prefer my bandits in the city, where there are policemen, and my skunks made into furs. If this is a peaceful country evening, I'm not strong enough for any more."

I believe even our dear Tish was shaken for the moment, especially when the man at the garage merely took one sniff and then refused to let the car inside the place. But he offered to turn a hose inside it as it stood outside the garage and let the water run the rest of the night, and at last we went home.

I must admit, however, that for some time after, we could see people on the sidewalks turn and sniff as we passed them in the street; and for several weeks dogs, of which Aggie is fond, would approach her in friendly fashion and then turn and run like all-possessed.

III

We did not go to the farm at once. Aggie had taken a heavy cold, due to scant apparel that night and to three or four baths every day for some time following. But the incident of the bandit and the lantern led to an unforeseen experience in the interval.

We were taking an evening drive to get some eggs from Jeremiah Tibbs, the caretaker at the farm, when we again saw a man waving a red lantern. This time, however, Tish did not stop. She stepped hard on the gas instead; the next instant there was a most terrible crash, and we went entirely through the side of a house that was being moved and which practically filled the road.

There was a complete and dreadful silence for a moment. Then the plaster dust began to settle and I could see where we were. We were inside the building, with the top of the car gone, but no other injuries; and a tall, nice-looking young man who had been frying bacon over a stove by the light of a candle was gazing at us with surprise.

"Well!" he said. "Welcome to our city! There is a door, but maybe you didn't notice it."

There was quite an excitement for a while; the man on the tractor which was pulling the building stating that the bump had broken his nose, and the man with the lantern stating that Tish had tried to run over him. In the end, however, matters quieted, although it required some time to extricate us, and I must say the young man behaved beautifully. He cooked us some more bacon while our car was being extricated, and, after coffee and a taste of the cordial which we always carry, even became quite talkative.

He was, he said, a writer by profession, and, as such, liked to carry his house with him.

"Matter of convenience," he said pleasantly. "Toothbrush always where it ought to be, and so on. The lowly turtle lives like that and seems to like it. Just now I got tired of where I was; same creek, same cows eating the geraniums—you get the idea, of course. So I decided to change the view. It's really very simple when you know how. The only drawback is that traveling in this manner is monotonous. The landscape changes too slowly."

Well, we were all pleased with him, and glad to find that he had rented a piece of meadow just below Tish's farm. He said his name was Bellamy, and seemed disappointed when we had never heard of him. He smiled, however, and merely observed that such is fame.

I thought Tish was rather thoughtful when at last we left, and it was some minutes before she spoke. Then she said grimly:

"Business must be good! At least he has bought a house."

"Some writers make money, Tish," I observed.

"Writer!" she said scornfully. "He is no writer. Lizzie, that is our bandit."

I must say I was shocked. But Tish is seldom wrong, and I had to admit that it was possible. Nor were our anxieties allayed when, on finally moving to the farm some days later, we saw that the moving house was firmly settled by the road where our lane entered it, and that the Bellamy man himself was sitting on the doorstep and waved to us.

There is also no doubt in my mind that the second incident that night contributed to our later misfortunes; for, on driving into the barnyard, a surprising sight met our eyes. The yard was filled with trucks, and from every one of them was coming such a squealing as I, for one, had never heard before. We were completely mystified, until at last the explanation came to us. They were pigs. There seemed to be hundreds of them, and as well as we could make out, the men were taking them out of the trucks and putting them into the empty sties, the barn, and even the fields. I shall never forget Jeremiah's face when he saw us.

"I thought you were coming next week," he said. "About these pigs now—"

"What about these pigs?" said Tish coldly.

"Well, it's like this, Miss Carberry," he said. "My brother's got a lot of pigs to ship to market, and it's a long haul. He asked if he could stop them here overnight and tomorrow, and I said he could. You see, a hog, he can stand just so much. Then he's got to have rest and food, like any other creature. Some people call them just hogs, but they've got feelings, Miss Carberry. They've got feelings."

This is the explanation of what followed, for the next afternoon a polite gentleman in a government car drove up, and we saw that Jeremiah tried to head him off from us; but after he had looked over the pigs and apparently tried to count them, he came up to the porch and asked Tish if she intended to keep all of them.

"Certainly not," she said. "I detest the creatures."

He looked rather surprised, but he smiled politely, and after Tish had told him that there wouldn't be a hog on the place by the next day, he went away.

Late that night we heard a number of trucks drive in, and by the squealing we gathered that Jeremiah's brother had come for his livestock. Not until long afterward did we discover that those hogs were being driven around the country at night just one jump ahead of the government inspector, and I take this occasion to state that any money Tish received from Washington as a result of that incident went at once to charity. But it is my opinion that Jeremiah Tibbs hated us from that time, and that it was he who got us into the trouble later on.

Well, we more or less settled down after that, although Hannah hated the place from the start. One rainy day I found her on the back porch, putting on her raincoat and overshoes and picking up her umbrella, and when she saw me she burst into tears.

We persuaded her to stay, however; and then, only a morning or two later, we saw the redheaded girl again. She stood for a time looking over a fence at us as we sat on the porch, knitting, and then leaped it like a boy and came up to us.

"Hello!" she said. "Welcome to the rural districts. How's the hog business?"

I must say she was pretty enough, if she did look like a forest fire; and if she had on anything but a pair of overalls and a green shirt, it was not noticeable. Tish asked her to sit down, so she perched on the edge of the porch and fished for a cigarette and matches.

"That's the advantage of pants," she said. "They've got pockets."

Then Aggie asked her if she had been troubled by the bandit lately, and she looked as nearly savage as a pretty girl can look.

"Troubled!" she said. "If that subnormal thinks he can trouble me, he'd better think again."

She said her name was Lelia Vaughn, and asked us earnestly if we thought she would be a good type for moving pictures. But outside of the fact that she was staying at one of the big houses below she gave no information.

As to the night she had met the bandit she was very reticent; merely observing that if she had a weapon she would shoot him on sight.

I must say we liked her. She had green eyes and a way of looking lonely and pathetic that touched all our hearts. And after that first call she came often. She even let Tish show her how to knit, although I must say the results were pretty terrible.

Then one morning, after she had had some cookies and a small glass of our cordial, she opened up and told us her tragic story.

"When I look at your kind faces," she said, "I feel that I can confide in you, and I must talk to somebody or go mad." Here she ate another cookie, and then resumed: "I know it will sound incredible. I know that I appear to be free as the air. But it is not true. Actually, I am a prisoner."

I recall that we all put down our knitting and stared at her.

"A prisoner!" Tish said. "What sort of prisoner?"

"For love," she said in a low voice. "I have been sent here so that I cannot see or communicate with the man I care for. And if you don't believe it, you might look down and see if there is a heavy-set creature who is an ex-prize fighter leaning against a fence somewhere."

There was! Far below, a man whom we had never seen before was smoking a pipe and staring in our direction, and Lelia gave a slow sad smile and went on.

"That gorilla," she said, "is my day jailer, and the man who shot at me is on duty at night. They have even taken away my car. "You are," she said tragically, "the only friends I have left in the world."

I shall never forget Tish's expression as she put down her knitting, or the tears in Aggie's eyes. Aggie had had a frustrated love affair of her own in early life, and ever since has been sympathetic with lovers. And Lelia must have seen our faces, for after that she told us her story. She was, she said, madly in love with a young man in the city whom she called Eddie—she never gave him any other name— and we gathered that he was also in love with her.

"But he is poor," she added dejectedly. "You know how it is these days. And my people have someone else in view. He is bald-headed and has a tummy, but he has plenty of money. So I am sent here, as my father puts it, to get my senses back."

Here she suddenly fumbled for a not-very-clean handkerchief and held it to her eyes.

"I'll never do it," she said. "Never. Let them

starve me. Let them beat me. Let them lock me up.
Can you imagine me marrying a man named Theodore, and having little Theodores all over the place?"

"It is incredible," Tish said slowly. "Such abuse
of power in this day and generation! How old are
you?"

Well, it seemed that she was nineteen, and that in
two years she would inherit quite a lot of money
from somebody; but what she wanted, she said, was
to get her money now, so that she could marry Eddie
at once and they could go west, probably to Hollywood, and start life all over again.

I must admit that we were profoundly touched.
Aggie, indeed, was weeping, and when Lelia had at
last made a dejected departure, I saw Tish watching
her as she crossed the fields.

"I came here for rest and peace," she said, "but injustice is injustice anywhere. If that story is true and
the child is indeed a prisoner, something should be
done. And soon."

I have quoted her exactly, as the press has never
published a withdrawal of many of the entirely false
statements made at the time. Our entire intention
was to prevent a grave miscarriage of justice; and
although I object to strong language, anyone who
says that we knew what was in that bag as it fell
from the sky lies in his teeth.

IV

For the next day or two Tish was not her calm and
usual self. It was in vain that Aggie baked a devil's-

food cake, for Tish did not touch it. It rained for two days, also, and so we did not see Lelia; but when it cleared on the second evening Tish suddenly proposed that we go down to the house where the girl was a prisoner and there test the truth of her story.

Aggie protested wildly, as she not only had taken a fresh cold but after her experience with the skunk she feared the nocturnal life of the fields. Tish, however, was firm, and at last we started out.

It was midnight when we left, and as, in order to avoid observation, Tish had left the lane and taken to the pastures, we moved but slowly. I am sorry to say that it was in our own lower meadow that Aggie had her unfortunate experience with the bull. We had quite forgotten that Jeremiah, some days before, had said that it would be necessary to borrow a bull for some purpose or other, and the first Tish and I knew of it was the sound of some creature moving about and pawing the ground with its feet. It was a dark night and we saw nothing, and suddenly we were almost paralyzed by Aggie's agonized voice.

"He's comig after be!" she yelled. "The bull! He's comig! Help!"

How can I record the horror of that moment, when we heard the enormous animal rushing across the meadow, an agonized final yelp from Aggie, and then the dull thud which could only be her poor body, thrown over the fence to land in the road! Or our relief when, on bending over her with a flashlight, we saw her open her eyes! But a moment later she sat up and, clapping her hands to her mouth, gave us a strange and dreadful look.

"I have thwallowed by teeth!" she said dully.

It was indeed a shocking moment, for she certainly did not have them. But she was otherwise uninjured, and I may say here that Jeremiah found both sets clear across the road the next morning and seemed highly suspicious when he handed them to us.

Obviously she could not go on with us, nor did she wish to do so. Instead, we propped her up in a fence corner and continued on to Lelia's house, which proved to be a large one in extensive grounds. And had we doubted the truth of the girl's story, we now had proof of it.

The Bellamy man was on guard under a tree, and as we watched from the shrubbery we heard a window open and Lelia's voice.

"Listen," she called down. "Do you have to whistle?   I need some sleep."

"Sweetheart!" he said cheerfully. "I just wanted you to know that I am here. You might be lonely, you know."

"Oh, stop it," she said in a tone of desperation. "I'm sick of seeing you. I'm sick of hearing you talk and hearing you whistle. I'm sick of the whole business."

"Well, I could sing," he suggested. "I have quite a good voice. People have come miles to hear me. It might pass the time."

That seemed to infuriate her, for she raised her voice. "All right," she said. "You think you've got a hard job now, don't you? Well, it isn't anything to what you are going to have. You'll be sorry you ever saw me."

He laughed at that, rather mockingly, I thought. "Sorry, sweetheart!" he said. "But I'm sorry now. I'm sorry for your disposition, which is mean and vicious, I'm sorry I can't spank you. And I'm sorry that I've got to stand out here instead of being in my own little bed. Look here. Throw me some cigarettes, will you? I've run out of them."

She left the window, and we both thought she meant to get the cigarettes. Evidently the Bellamy man did too, for he moved closer and stood waiting. The next moment, however, there was a terrific crash, as though a chair had dropped on him, and we could hear him swearing and her voice from above.

"Good night, darling," she called, and slammed the window.

It was then that Tish and I took a careful departure. Whatever one might think of Lelia's actions, as Tish observed, there was now no doubt whatever that she had told us the truth.

We found Aggie somewhat recovered in her fence corner and took her home, and, as I have said, Jeremiah found her teeth clear across the road the next morning. She was still in bed at the time, and he stalked into the dining room and laid them on the breakfast table.

"By and large," he said, "I've picked up quite a few things on that road. Empty bottles and such like. But darned if I ever found a full set of teeth, uppers and lowers." He then stared hard at both Tish and myself, and said there were queer things going on and that honest folks stayed in their beds at night.

I think I may safely say that the change in Tish dated from that time. She had long, absorbed moments when, her knitting neglected on her lap, she sat staring down toward where Lelia was being kept under surveillance, and others when she took long excursions alone into the mountains. Then one evening she drew Aggie and me aside and said that, in view of certain possible emergencies, she had been looking for a shelter in the hills, and that at last she had found it.

"A shelter from what?" said Aggie, turning pale.

Tish eyed her gravely.

"The time may come," she said, "when it will be necessary to rescue Lelia from her captors—for such they evidently are—and to open up for her a new and independent life. At such a time I hope I shall not fail in my duty as I see it. Do you want to see her forced to marry this Theodore?"

Well, none of us did, for that matter; and a day or so later Tish took us to see the cabin. It was certainly hidden, and it was in fair condition, with built-in bunks and a lean-to kitchen with a stove.

After that for some days we were busily—if stealthily—engaged in putting it to rights, and at last one night we carried up a considerable amount of canned food and left it there. Unfortunately, we had no means of transportation, and so Tish, with her usual acumen, used one of the house shutters for the purpose. I shall always consider it a real misfortune that we forgot the shutter and left it there, for Jeremiah missed it the next morning, and I never saw a face so suspicious as his when he reported it to us.

"Man and boy," he said, "I've seen quite a few things stole. But a shutter, now! A pair of shutters, that's one thing. But one shutter! Only use I can think of for one shutter is to carry a body on."

Well, there was no body, of course; but about that time somebody found the clothing Aggie had discarded in the field the night she met the skunk, and what with Jeremiah finding her teeth in the road and now the shutter, the story got about that a woman had been murdered in the vicinity and her body disposed of somehow. As a result, we actually had a visit from the sheriff of the county a few days later. He said he had merely looked in to see how we were getting along, but it was plain that he was suspicious of us, and I saw him take a long look into the well before he left.

It was indeed that very night that, all of us having retired, we heard a terrific pounding on the front door; and that Tish, armed with Charlie Sands' shotgun, went down and threw it open.

On the doorsteps was Lelia, still in her overalls and panting for breath, and when she had rushed in and locked the door, she simply dropped into a chair and closed her eyes.

"The dirty something or other!" she said. "He chased me!"

We gave her some cordial, and soon she was herself again. All she had wanted to do, she said, was to take a moonlight ride, and so she had managed to get out of the house and steal the key to Mr. Bellamy's car from his cabin. There was, however, something wrong with the starter, and so he had heard her. She had just got the engine going when he leaped on the running board.

"All I had time to do," she said, "was to head it for the ditch and then jump and run, with him after me. He would have got me too," she said drearily, "but for that bull in the lower field. It made for him, and that gave me a chance. Otherwise—"

She made a pathetic gesture, and I must say my heart went out to her.

It was that night that Tish told her about the cabin and how to reach it. I wish to state here that none of us suggested that she attempt to reach it; least of all that she should take along Charlie Sands' shotgun. These she did on her own initiative, and the statement that we taped her eyes and mouth is simply absurd. As to the bottle of chloroform found later in Tish's apartment, it was used for the bat and for no other purpose.

Our sole contribution to that night was to tuck her into a comfortable bed, where she lay looking at us with a soft sad smile.

"I am so grateful," she said gently. "And how strange to think that you three are my only friends."

That was the last time either Aggie or I saw her for five days, and any assertion to the contrary is blatantly false.

V

I rose the next day at my usual hour and was somewhat astonished to find young Bellamy sitting on the front porch and cheerfully smiling.

"Good morning," he said. "And how is our little friend this morning? Not too weary, I trust."

I could only eye him with disfavor. He looked muddy—from which I gathered that the bull had given him some trouble—but entirely calm.

"I am surprised that you dare to ask that," I said coldly.

He only smiled again.

"Why not?" he said. "I assure you that my interest in her is extreme. In fact," he added with a change of tone, "if I ever lay my hands on that red-headed brat again, I'll teach her a few things. I'll teach her to throw chairs on me," he went on with increasing bitterness. "And other furniture. Would you believe that in the past few weeks she has dumped practically everything portable in that house on me at night, including a pair of brass book ends? They were heads of George Washington, at that. Where's her patriotism? Where's her humanity? Where's— Oh, what's the use? Where is she?"

Tish came to the front door at that moment, and I saw at once that she looked weary, as though she had not slept, but at the sight of the Bellamy man she was her old self again. She at once ordered him off the farm, but he shook his head.

"Not without my little friend," he said.

It was then that Tish took advantage of the situation to tell him what she thought of him, and of his endeavor to ruin a young life; I must say he looked startled, especially when she came to the love story. Indeed, toward the end he was sitting on the porch steps, holding his head in his hands. When he finally looked up, he had a haunted look in his eyes.

"I see," he said. "Eddie, of course. And Theodore, naturally. There weren't any more that you can remember?"

"She seemed to consider the two quite adequate," Tish observed icily.

He got up then and stared out over the countryside.

"Adequate," he repeated, as though to himself. "Adequate is the word. Completely and entirely adequate. I've been trying to think of that word for the past six weeks."

He did not explain further, but demanded at least to talk to the girl; and as there was nothing else to be done, I went to waken her. To my horror, she was not there, and as the windows were open it did not require much intelligence to see that she had escaped by the shed roof.

Well, I must say that the Bellamy man went crazy when I told him. He insisted on searching the house, and when at last he departed it was to say that if we had a hand in her disappearance we would go to the penitentiary for life.

"Either you've got her hidden," he said furiously, "or she's down the road somewhere looking pitiful, so some sap will pick her up and take her into town. But I warn you, I'm suspicious. I'm suspicious as hell. And if God ever forgives me for taking this job—"

He jammed his hat onto his head and departed in a shocking temper.

It was after he had gone that Tish told Aggie and me that Lelia was undoubtedly safe and sound in the cabin, with Charlie Sands' shotgun to protect her, and that we must enable her to get in touch with Eddie as soon as possible. Before we were able to do so it became entirely impossible. It seemed to us that Mr. Bellamy had barely departed when both the house and the farm were entirely covered with policemen, from state troopers on motorcycles to the man Aggie found when she went to look for eggs, lying in the hayloft of the barn and watching the house with a pair of field glasses.

Not only that, but the same afternoon we had a most unpleasant visit from the sheriff.

"What I want to say is this," he remarked: "This has always been a law-abiding county, until lately. Now what have we got? Clothes in a field, but no body; two sets of teeth, a missing shutter, and a lost girl. For two cents I'd drag that well of yours."

"I wish you would," said Tish coldly. "One of Jeremiah's cats has been gone for a week."

He gave her an ugly look.

"And so, I understand, is a shotgun which was formerly your property," he said grimly.

Well, I must say I never saw so much excitement about a missing girl in my life. As Tish observed, probably her parents had been caught in the crash and it was necessary for her to make a wealthy marriage. Nevertheless, we were the chief sufferers. There we were, with about as much privacy as canary birds, so that more than once I found Hannah again in tears on the back porch; and with no way whatever to get to Lelia and the cabin. And this continued for five days. Indeed, had it not been for Tish's resourcefulness, we would probably be there yet. But, as usual, she finally brought the keenness of her fertile mind to our predicament.

"I have noticed," she said, "that these observers pay no attention to us when we emerge with the egg baskets in full daylight, although at night every door and window is watched. Our escape must, therefore, be through the henhouse."

It is thus that I explain for the first time the mystery which so puzzled both press and state and county police at the time.

The matter, indeed, proved extremely simple. One at a time and at sufficient intervals each of us carried an egg basket to the henhouse and remained there; and at dusk Tish with a chisel carefully pried off one or two of the bands at the rear.

As the henhouse backed on thick shrubbery which, in turn, led to the woods, at dusk that night we found ourselves free at last. Not only that, but we had a dozen fresh eggs to carry to the cabin, which were greatly appreciated later.

The climb through the timber was not easy. It was a dark and moonless night, and Aggie insisted that there were bears all around us. Tish finally was driven to remonstrate with her.

"For heaven's sake, show some sense, Aggie," she

said. "A bear runs at the mere sight of any human being."

"Which way does he run?" Aggie quavered.

But this colloquy came to an end by our arrival at the small clearing around the cabin, and the discovery that there was a light in it. Even Aggie was cheered. But the next moment, to our horror and amazement, there was the sound of a shot from within it, followed in a second by another.

How can I express our feelings at that moment? Aggie was whimpering beside me, and even Tish was startled. Then, telling us to remain where we were, she moved cautiously forward to where she could peer into one of the windows. When she came back, she was very grave.

"It is Lelia," she said. "She is in there alone, and I think she has gone mad."

We all then crept to the window, and I shall never forget the picture we saw. One candle had been lighted, the door to the lean-to kitchen was closed and had a chair against it, and in the center of the room stood the poor child, clad just as she had left us, and hastily reloading Charlie Sands' shotgun. Her eyes looked quite frenzied, and even as we gazed she lifted the gun and prepared to fire again.

Never in my life have we faced such a situation. Apparently loneliness and despair had affected her mind, and we at once withdrew to survey the situation.

"The only thing to do," Tish said, "is to surround her and capture her before she can shoot again. It is possible that she is only temporarily deranged, and that under proper care she will recover."

She then outlined her plan. Aggie was to enter the dark kitchen and lock the door, thus preventing Lelia's escape in that direction; I was to signal from outside a window when she turned her back to the door, and Tish—our valiant Tish—was then to enter and seize the gun, when we would all close in.

I must say that Aggie was most unwilling, but at last we saw her disappear around the corner of the cabin, and I went to my window. At that moment I heard strange noises from beyond the door to the kitchen—a sort of scratching, followed by the impact of a heavy body against it—and before we could shout, Lelia had raised the gun and fired directly at it!

What happened then was indescribable. There was a terrific roar from the kitchen and a thin wail from Aggie. And then silence!

I can only remember Tish dashing open the door, and Lelia staring at us with blank eyes.

"There's a bear in the kitchen," she said. "I haven't had anything to eat for three days."

Then she dropped the gun and slid to the floor in a faint.

Never, so long as I live, will I forget that moment, with Lelia apparently unconscious and Aggie shut in with that wild and savage brute. Nor did repeated calls to her bring more than furious lunges by the animal at the door. I recall that Tish hurried around to the outer door of the lean-to, but, obedient to instructions, Aggie had locked it.

There was but one thing to do, and that was to let the animal out through the cabin. This we finally did, putting Lelia in an upper bunk and taking refuge there ourselves after opening the door an inch or two. It was hideous to see the creature poke its nose into that aperture and gradually emerge into the room; but, at that moment I heard the happiest sound of my life: Aggie suddenly sneezed, and the animal bolted out the open door and was gone.

We found Aggie on the floor behind the kitchen stove, and apparently unharmed. But we could not induce her to come out.

"Don't be a fool, Aggie," Tish said sharply. "Get out of there. The creature's gone."

"Gode?" said our poor Aggie in a weak voice. "Thed what is sittig od by feet?"

Well, we brought the candle then and looked, and there was a bear cub, and a fairly good-sized one at that. It seemed quite friendly, and as though it would have wagged its tail if had had one; but at last we got it out and were able to get Aggie to a bunk.

I am glad to say that after a good supper of fresh eggs and bacon, with some waffles which I stirred up, Lelia was quite herself again. It appeared that she had reached the cabin safely and that for two days all had gone well. Then on the third, while she was sleeping, the bear and the cub had got into the kitchen and in some manner the door had latched behind them.

However, all is well that ends well, and, save that Aggie claimed that a field mouse had sat on her chest for hours and washed its face, we put in a comfortable night.

I can only add that this was the "inhuman captivity" to which the press later referred!

VI

Lelia was in excellent spirts the next morning, and over the breakfast table proposed a plan. This was that she walk to a town of which she knew across the mountain and there telephone to Eddie.

Tish wished to accompany her, but she insisted on going alone, and at last she departed, wearing a bandanna of Aggie's to hide her red hair, and with— as Tish observed—the light of hope in her young face. She had no more than gone when we heard a scrambling among some rocks and turned to see the Bellamy man climbing up the trail.

It was a real shock, but I felt almost sorry for him. He looked as though he had not slept for a week, and it was not until he had searched the cabin and we had told him about the bear that he was convinced of our innocence and apologized.

"All right," he said dejectedly. "She wins. If there was a bear here, and she saw it, she'd have it doing tricks for her and eating out of her hand." And he added in a gloomy voice: "Some of these days I'll end by believing that story of hers myself. I feel it coming on. I'm weakening. Either that or she's smarter than I am. You can take your choice."

He then took up his hat and prepared to go. At the top of the path, however, he stopped.

"Just in case you happen to see her," he said, "you can tell her for me that I'm through, and that I'm going back to my regular job. It's easy. It's simple. I can understand professionals. Either you get them or they get you. But these amateurs—"

Here he checked himself, and soon after that he was out of sight, leaving us rather puzzled, but relieved. As Tish said at the time, under other conditions one could have liked him very much. He had a pleasant smile and was quite good-looking. But with things as they were—

Nothing else occurred that day, although Aggie, on her way to the spring, slipped and sat down on a porcupine and was most uncomfortable for some time. Lelia returned safely by evening, looking tired but quite contented, and ate a ravenous supper. She explained that she had got Eddie on the telephone and arranged with him to secure some clothing for her and a moderate sum of money and to hire a plane and drop them, packed in a small bag, at a point in the hills to be indicated by a white sheet laid out on the ground. We were then to gather up bag and sheet, and there would be nothing to indicate the spot.

Once properly dressed and with adequate funds, she was to meet Eddie and then determine on their future course.

This is the co-called villainous plot, laid to Letitia Carberry's door and called by the ugly name of extortion. And it is worthy of note that, while our arrest for it covered the front pages of the papers, the refutation was hidden among the advertising matter.

But to go back. Lelia was quite firm about the sheet, but there was nothing of the sort at the camp, and as the plane was to arrive the following day, it fell to my lot to go down to the farm that night and secure one.

It was indeed a painful and arduous journey, especially in view of the bear. Also, Hannah had locked the house carefully, and in the end I was compelled to break a window in order to enter. This wakened her, and as I had no wish to be recognized I was obliged to wrap myself in the sheet and make my escape as best I could.

This, I may say here, is the origin of the ghost story which still persists in the neighborhood, and I am happy to lay at rest.

However, I found everything ready on my return, and long before daylight we were on our way. Necessarily our progress was slow, owing to the dark and to no path whatever, but by daylight we had covered several miles and were quite ready for our breakfast of broiled ham, toast, and coffee.

We rested for a brief time and then started again, and it was not until noon that Tish paused. We were on the top of a mountain where a lumbering company had cut some timber, and a chute led far down the mountainside and out of sight, and Tish surveyed it carefully.

"This, I think," she observed, "answers all requirements. It is open to the sky, and we can remain sheltered among the trees. We can eat a light lunch, and by that time the plane should be here."

This we did, and after spreading the sheet we rested our weary bodies. I can still remember the sun on Lelia's bright head, and Tish's statement that we were on a crusade and that if any trouble developed we could take to the chute and slide to safety. Then I must have slept, for when I wakened it was almost dusk, and Aggie was shaking me by the shoulder and sneezing wildly.

"It's coming, Lizzie," she said. "I cad hear it."

Well, we at once retired to our places in the woods, and soon the plane was overhead. It seemed suspicious at first, for it circled several times. Then it came lower, and soon we saw the bag tossed overboard. To our horror, however, it missed the sheet entirely and fell among the trees instead.

It never struck the ground at all.

It was some time before we discovered it. For one thing, Lelia, running toward us, had fallen and sprained her ankle, and we were obliged to look after her first. But at last we saw it, hanging to a branch far up in a tree and utterly beyond our reach.

Lelia sat on the ground and stared at it furiously.

"The fools!" she said. "The blithering idiots! They did it on purpose."

She refused to explain further, and as evening was now falling rapidly our problem had become acute.

With her injured ankle, Lelia could not climb the tree, and at last Tish suggested that Aggie, being the lightest among us, should go up and bring down the bag. I shall never forget poor Aggie's face.

"Clibe that tree?" she asked. "What do you thik I ab? A skyrocket?"

In the end, however, she agreed—although none too willingly—and at last we succeeded in hoisting her to a lower limb. For some time we could hear her moving upward, until she was far above us; and then suddenly we heard the stealthy sounds of movement all about us, and realized that we were surrounded!

How shall I relate what followed? The shocking sight of Mr. Bellamy, red-faced and raging, catching our unfortunate Lelia and deliberately turning her over and—I hesitate to relate this—spanking her violently; my own fingers closing without intention on both barrels of the shotgun, and an explosion which threw me flat and knocked out a pivot tooth, followed by a yelp from a state trooper; and as I went down, a brief vision of Tish pushing at the sheriff as he tried to lay hands on her; and his sudden disappearance into the timber chute—those are the pictures which rise in my mind as I write this, and bitter indeed they are.

Somewhere above us in a tree were Aggie and the bag, but I could see neither of them; nor in that long walk and, later, ride to the county jail did either Tish or I mention them. We were handcuffed, and to this crowning indignity Tish made no protest.

"If it is a crime," she said, "to bring young lives together, then I am indeed a criminal!"

We saw nothing more of the sheriff, although we

learned later that, the chute ending in the river, he had had a most unpleasant experience. But one thing puzzled us both. This was their insistence that we had hidden the bag from the plane, and that it contained a huge sum of money. Not, indeed, until after Charlie Sands had come and gone the next day had we the slightest comprehension of what they meant. Then I looked out to see him standing beyond the bars of our cell.

"Well," he said, "I guess you are beyond help this time."

"I don't even know what you are talking about," said Tish. "If I have tried to help a pair of young lovers, that is entirely my affair. I have committed no felony."

"Maybe not in this state," he said coldly, "but in some parts of this great and glorious Union shooting at a sheriff and then filling him full of splinters is not regarded with any favor."

"He slipped," said Tish calmly.

"He says you pushed him," Charlie Sands retorted. "I've been in to see him, and he has two constables and a deputy working over him with tweezers."

It was some time before he could induce her to tell him the story, and when she had finished he simply held on to the bars and stared at her.

"I see," he said rather feebly. "Of course, it's quite simple. The cruel parents and the sweet young thing to be saved. And Eddie and Theodore. And Aggie still in a tree with a bag dropped from a plane. What could be more natural? I say," he added, "you haven't a spot of blackberry cordial about, have you? I feel rather queer."

He went away soon after that, and I believe that Aggie was rescued later that day by some fire department or other which carried up a long ladder. They found the bag also, and it contained fifty thousand dollars in small bills, and no clothing whatever.

It was the ransom money for Edith Lee, and Lelia had been Edith Lee all the time! Moreover, although we did not know it then, she had merely invented all the attempts to kidnap her, in order to get money so she could go into motion pictures; and Mr. Bellamy and the man with the pipe had been not her jailers, but guards to protect her.

It was late that evening that Mr. Bellamy came to the cell to see us and was admitted. He sat down as though he was very tired and for some time merely examined his hands, which appeared to be badly scratched.

"Someday," he said at last, "some good strong man is going to take that redhead and beat Hollywood out of her. Then he'll probably marry her and live happily ever after. But I am not the man. Theodore might have done it; I don't know. But not Eddie. I never cared for Eddie. With a mind like hers, she should have done better with Eddie. In my opinion Eddie was a washout."

"Was?" said Tish in a dreadful voice. "Has anything happened to him."

"My dear lady," he said, "Eddie has passed into limbo again, as has Theodore. They lived their short but eventful lives wholly in her mind, and if Providence is good to me I shall go back to Washington and hand in my resignation. Anyone who could fall for a girl like that isn't safe to be let loose."

He then got up and gave a sort of groan. "The right man," he said heavily, "could make something of her. But I've got my fingers crossed."

Well, it turned out that he was actually a G-man or something of the sort, and when the Lee girl made up her story about kidnapers and her people hid her in the country he had been sent to watch her. But he never had believed that story, and I must say for her that when they got Aggie and the bag she told the truth for once, and we were released that night.

We went at once to the farm, to find our poor Aggie with her cold much worse and using language she had never used before.

"It was all right for you," she said bitterly. "You were id a dice warb cell. But I was id a tree, with a policemad udder be, tryig to look like a dabbed bird! If you thik that's fuddy, go ad try it."

She was very resentful, as the policeman had not moved from her vicinity all night; and once she had had to sneeze, and he whipped out his revolver. After that, every now and then she had had to make a noise like a bird, for he was evidently suspicious. The worst trouble she had, however, was with a squirrel. It got used to her after a time, she said, and was evidently nesting, as little by little it bit off most of her new switch and carried it away.

Nothing would induce her to stay at the farm after that, and so we spent the remainder of the spring and summer in the city. But that fall we had a great surprise. We received an invitation to Lelia's —or I should say Edith Lee's—wedding; she was marrying the Bellamy man, after all!

We went to the church, and I must say she made a beautiful bride. Under her veil her hair did not seem as red as usual, but she had not entirely changed; for, coming down the aisle just beside our pew, Mr. Bellamy stepped on her dress and she said something under her breath.

He never stopped smiling, but all of us saw him give her arm quite a dreadful pinch, and Charlie Sands, who was sitting with us, leaned over and spoke to Tish.

"Don't worry about them," he said. "She's under control. Everything's under control from now on." . . .

Well, that is the story. I have felt it necessary to tell it in detail, as one of the smart-aleck national magazines has recently referred to our dear Tish as "whilom kidnaper, Letitia Carberry." This is most unfair, as it was Edith Lee herself—pretending to be Lelia Vaughn—who, while professing to get in touch with an Eddie who did not exist, called her anxious parents by telephone and said that she had been kidnaped. It was her idea about the sheet and the ransom money also; and I have always regarded it as outrageous that the sheriff sent us a bill for a new suit of clothes and for medical attention, including the removal of certain splinters from his person.

We have all recovered, save, perhaps, Aggie. She

has been subject to nightmares ever since, and her nerves are not what they were. Once or twice at night I have found her standing up in her bed, clutching a bedpost and uttering a sort of feeble peep-peep, as though she were a bird.

But, as I have intimated, the whole affair has left Tish with a definite complex as to red lanterns. As a result, only a few days ago she drove past one at night, to discover too late that she had driven onto a large hoist which was carrying building materials to the upper stories of a new structure that was being erected.

It did not pause until it had reached the sixteenth floor, and as work ceased at that time, we were left there all night.

I shall never forget the expressions of the men on the ground when we were lowered there the next morning and drove away. But I shall also always remember Charlie Sands' face when he brought in the evening paper.

"I am not a betting man," he said, "but if you will tell me you were not the three women who spent last night in a car on top of the steel work of the new Standard Building, I will not only go to church next Sunday, I will put ten dollars on the plate."

There was nothing to do but to tell him, and over a glass of blackberry cordial he regarded us, one after the other.

"I shall go to church anyhow," he said solemnly.

THE OYSTER

THE OYSTER

I

IT WAS last March that Tish, on her way home from church, picked up the Florida picture section of the morning paper and there saw a picture of an enormous fish. It was leaping out of the water, and a tired-looking man in a boat the size of the fish had a death grip on a rod, and had torn one sleeve out of his shirt.

Tish put down the paper thoughtfully.

"It is a curious thing," she observed, "how little we know of the depths of the sea. We sail over it; ever and anon we bathe in it. But what does it contain? What goes on in its awful depths?"

"I don't know, and what's more, I don't care," said Aggie positively. "So far as I'm concerned any old thing can go on."

Tish was not listening. It is characteristic of her that her logical mind, once seizing on a subject, pursues it relentlessly.

"Again," she went on, "what do we know of the southern portion of our country? Of the old historic South? Nothing. Nothing at all."

"True," said Aggie, "and plenty goes on there too, I understand. If you're leading up to Florida, Tish Carberry—"

But Tish had taken up the paper and was again gazing at the fish.

" 'Diamond-button tarpon,' " she read, " 'making its fourteenth leap.' Unless that's a double negative picture, that is a real fish, Lizzie. That man got a diamond button for getting it."

"A diamond button!" Aggie said. "What good did a diamond button do him? What he needed was a bottle of liniment and a new shirt. And who wants one diamond button anyhow? If it was a dozen, or even a half dozen, it would mean something."

Tish explained to her that it was a decoration, to be worn like the ribbon of the Croix de Guerre, but Aggie was unconvinced. Unlike Tish, who is rather radical in temperament, Aggie is a conservative, in addition to suffering badly from hay fever.

"I'm not going south," she said flatly. "It may mean a diamond button to you, but it only means hay fever to me."

It was quite clear to me, however, that Tish had already made up her mind to go south. She cut out the picture and placed it in her reticule, and before she left she gave Aggie a little talk on the advantages of sea air on the mucous passages of the nose, and also on the cry of the human skin for the rays of the sun.

"We wear too many clothes," she said. "There are four million pores in the human body, and what do we do with them? Clothe them!"

But Aggie was still mutinous.

"My pores are my own private business," she observed sulkily. And when Tish went on to speak of hours to be spent in the actinic rays of the sun on some sequestered beach, she said acidly that the sun gave her prickly heat, and that personally she preferred hay fever.

"I can *blow* my nose," she added tartly.

Nor was she impressed when, a day or so later, Tish sent us a quantity of literature issued by the railroads and steamship companies. These showed beautiful islands with palm trees and oranges on them, and a great many people with practically nothing on them at all. I can still see our poor Aggie staring at those pictures, ignorant of what was to come, and declaring emphatically that only her Maker had ever seen her like that or ever would.

But in the end the literature had its effect, and we began to plan to go south.

It was at this time that Charlie Sands paid Tish a visit, and in view of his bitterness since, I consider it well to set down that conversation.

He was very low-spirited at the beginning. He said that there was to be a new managing editor appointed on his paper, and that if the boss knew his business he, Charlie Sands, would get the job.

"I've been working my fool head off," he said. "I've even been taking Clara out, and if you knew Clara—!"

"Clara?"

"The daughter," he explained. "I've been taking her to night clubs all night, and working all day. She likes to go." Here he groaned. "Go! If you'd fasten a pedometer to that girl you'd find she travels about thirty miles every night around a dance floor. Believe me, when and if I land this job I'm going to bed for a week."

Here he yawned, and said that that was enough of Clara; he never had liked her, and now he was fed up and running over, and bankrupt into the bargain.

"I've got so that when I hear her voice on the telephone I dig in and get the good old wallet," he said.

Over a glass or two of blackberry cordial, however, he relaxed and grew more cheerful. It was then that Tish spoke of the Florida plan.

"It *sounds* all right," he said thoughtfully. "I can't see a hole in it at the moment. But in the light of past experience I feel that there is a hole, and that you'll get into it. There always has been, and you always have."

"Nonsense!" said Tish. "A simple vacation, with a bit of fishing!"

"You couldn't be induced to do a bit of liquor running from the West Indies?"

As Tish belongs to practically all the dry organizations in the country she met this with silence, and he poured himself another glass of cordial.

"Well," he said, "happy days, and wire me if you get into trouble."

Who could have foretold that when trouble did come, as it did, it would be impossible to wire him? Or to wire anybody?

He was feeling very cheerful when he left, and said that the boss was going to Florida too.

"Be good to him if you happen on him," he said. "He isn't a bad sort, although savage at times. But if you see him, remember the job and cherish him. Make him happy. Feed his vanity. And when you've got him where you want him, mention *me."*

I confess that this conversation made no great impression on me, being driven out of my mind by our preparations for departure. Tish had decided on a nice island on the west coast, with a good hotel and near two tarpon passes. There were many other islands about, as we verified by the map in the encyclopedia, and the passes led out in the Gulf of Mexico. In the spring the tarpon come in through these passes to lay their eggs, and later on we met a young man who said he had seen them doing it. They scrape a hole in the beach with their flippers, he said, and then lay the eggs. But while doing so they weep copiously. He had seen a very large one with tears streaming down its face.

One of the first things we did, I remember, was to purchase our fishing tackle. It appeared that for catching large fish it was necessary to have not only a stout pole, as they fight to free themselves, but a strong line and spool, or reel, with which to wind them in. Also that with this equipment went a sort of harness, made of leather and swung from the shoulders, and very much like the things used to carry flags in processions, in that it had a socket in front in which to rest the end of the pole.

The young man behind the counter was very affable. When Tish looked at the line and doubted its strength, he smiled and said it would bring in anything but a whale. Aggie sneezed violently at that, as some time before, while boating in the ocean, we had dropped our anchor and a fluke had caught in the blowhole of one of these great mammals. At first, when we began to move, I recall that Tish had mentioned the velocity of the tide. But it was not the tide, and the whale towed us for miles before finally blowing out the anchor.

"Now, just to show you how strong that line is," he said, "only the other day a friend of mine was fishing off the center of the railroad bridge, when a tug came along. Well, that meant raising the center span, so my friend just tied his line there and left it. Pretty soon he heard a lot of shouting, and he looked over. And what do you think? As the span raised, his hook had caught in the belt worn by the tug captain, and there he was, forty feet in the air and the tug going on without him."

"What size of man was he?" Tish inquired.

"Big heavy man. Must have weighed all of two hundred pounds."

"But of course he wasn't fighting. These fish *fight*. I understand."

"Wasn't fighting! I can tell you this. That captain almost bit a girder in two, and when they cut him down and he'd swum out, he about ruined this friend of mine. He's getting about now, but he's still on crutches."

Our dear Tish did not trouble to explain, and armed with our purchases we departed.

For purposes of comfort Tish had planned that our fishing costumes were to consist of our one-piece bathing suits, shameful contraptions with practically no lower portion whatever, but over which we were each to wear a long skirt for decency in the boat, and a mackintosh when leaving the hotel. And in view of later developments I must explain that we were to have a boat, but no boatman, Tish having had considerable experience in this line; dating indeed from the time at Lake Penzance when she was taking her first lesson, and started with such an unexpected jerk that she threw out the instructor.

I have never forgotten that incident, as she did not then know how to stop the engine, and we were obliged to cruise about at top speed for twenty-one hours, before the gasoline gave out.

Our preparations, however, were delayed by a most unfortunate occurrence. Or rather two of them.

About a week before our date of departure Hannah called us up in the middle of the night and asked us to go right over.

"What on earth *is* it, Hannah?" I asked.

"I don't know," she said tearfully. "She's locked in her room and groaning something awful. Every now and then I can hear her get out of bed and run in and turn on the shower bath, but she won't let me in."

Well, we dressed as fast as we could, and matters were as Hannah had said. The shower bath was running, and apparently Tish was in it, as she gave no heed to my knock.

"Tish!" Aggie cried. "Tish!"

In the end we decided to climb the fire escape and thus gain access to her, and this we did. But I shall never forget our horror when at last we stood outside her window and peered in through the pane.

The room was in a state of confusion, and our dear Tish, in practically a state of nature, was half running about it. Even as we gazed she shot with incredible rapidity into the bathroom, and we could hear the shower running again.

We got through the window somehow, and could hear Hannah outside in the hall.

"Here's the olive oil, Miss Tish," she was quavering. "And some baking soda and a lump of ice. If you'd only let me in—!"

It was not until Tish was in bed, her swollen face and portions of her poor body eased with oil and soda, that we learned what had happened. With her usual foresightedness she had bought a sun machine, in order to inure herself against the actinic rays of the South, and although carefully instructed to expose herself but two minutes at the beginning, had dropped asleep!

Toward dawn, under the medicinal influence of a quantity of blackberry cordial, she fell asleep, and we stole away.

But it was several days before she was quite herself again; although the weather was cold, she could not don her flannels for some time, as the itching was very unpleasant.

The second incident was most unfortunate, as for a time it appeared that our poor Aggie would give up the trip altogether.

It had been Tish's wise decision that, as we intended to be on the water most of the time and as boats were liable to accident, we should all take some swimming lessons. Aggie objected at once, and it was necessary to argue with her at great length.

"Water," Tish said, "is a friendly element, not an unfriendly one. A large part of the human body is water; a large part of the earth's surface is covered with water. Without water, where are we?"

"We're right here," said Aggie stubbornly. "Right here on good solid earth, and here I stay."

But in the end she agreed to make the experiment. Although she refused to go into the pool beyond the shallow end, we did succeed in getting her to stoop and wet her shoulders. But the lesson was not a great success for any of us. Even Tish found the buoyancy of water rather less than she had expected, and gave up trying to learn the Australian crawl stroke in favor of learning to keep her head above water.

All in all, I think we were rather discouraged when the instructor departed and we left the pool. And it was then that the second incident occurred to which I have referred. Aggie was behind us, and I had taken off my suit and was standing under a shower when I heard a splash, accompanied by a shriek. As quickly as possible I threw a bath towel around me and rushed out, to see the form of our beloved comrade drifting aimlessly beneath the surface. What was my relief, however, to perceive that she was quite conscious, and that she was holding her nose with one hand while struggling with the other! Tish had by that time reached me, in time to see Aggie rise to the surface, draw a deep breath, take a fresh grip of her nostrils and submerge again with a look of black indignation at both of us.

"She will not drown, Lizzie," Tish reassured me. "With that system she can go down almost indefinitely."

Fortunately the swimming instructor arrived soon after, and marking by the bubbles which arose the spot where she had last gone down, he rescued her at once. She was none the worse for her experience, although she sneezed steadily for an hour and a half. The only serious result was that she said she was through with water forever.

"Dever agaid," she said, as we stood about her. "Dever. I dod't give a dab if I dever go fishig. Let the fish stay id the water, if they dod't dow ady better. If they did dow better they wold'dt be fish."

After a glass or two of blackberry cordial, however, she improved greatly, although she said she was still dizzy from her experience. One of the phases of her recovery was that she insisted that she could not focus her eyes and was seeing everything double. As a matter of fact, Tish shortly after heard her sneezing violently in her dressing room, and found her surveying her shoes tearfully.

"I'be got four shoes ad four feet, Tish," she wailed, "ad I'be all bixed up."

Later on she was able to tell her story quite clearly. She said she had stepped on a wet cake of soap at the end of the diving board, and had been shot the length of the board and into the water before she could even scream.

Our preparations now went on apace. A day or

so later Charlie Sands telephoned to Tish that he'd been talking to the boss about tarpon, and that it was heavy work to land one, and needed muscle as well as practice. Also he said that the boss would be in our vicinity, and to look out for him.

"And no fooling!" he said. "Remember that he's bread and butter and payday to me, and watch over him. And if you can't get friendly," he added, "at least keep out of his way. I'd like to feel that he was safe anyhow. I need him in my business."

"Safe?" said Tish indignantly. "Do you think I intend to damage the man?"

"Absolutely not. But all I ask is this: if you feel an attack of trouble coming on, just leave him out of it. Pick on somebody else. That's all."

But—and I wish him to recall this—neither then nor at any other time did he describe the boss or give us his name. No matter how bitter he may feel he must do us this simple justice.

II

During the next few days we completed our arrangements. Tish shipped down a box of groceries and a case of bottled water in case, as she said, that we became attached to a large fish and were delayed after meal hours. Also we sent the wool with which we usually knit, during our vacations, the slippers et cetera for the Old Ladies' Home. And in leisure moments at Tish's request we practiced strengthening the muscles of arm and hand, as Charlie Sands had suggested.

Thus, Aggie turned the clothes wringer an hour or so each day, while I ran the lawn mower. Tish, living in an apartment, was able to attach a pair of flatirons to her line, and from the fire escape platform reel them in and thus exercise precisely the muscles required.

Unluckily, owing to the attitude of the people in the apartments below, she was compelled to do this work at night. They had never quite forgiven the fact that, some years before, during practice with a target in the cellar, she had accidentally sent a bullet up through the floor of the apartment above and struck a card table where some people named Johnson were playing bridge, and where Mr. Johnson had just doubled four no-trumps.

After she had done her fishing practice successfully from the fire escape for one or two nights, that had to be abandoned because a man named Jamieson, trying to get into his apartment rather late without waking Mrs. Jamieson, unfortunately saw the irons hanging there, and feeling rather cheerful he gave them a shove.

Well, of course they came back and struck him, and he went through a large windowpane and fell onto the dog, and Tish said the noise was really something frightful.

The janitor came up to see her the next morning, and he was most disagreeable.

"No," he said unpleasantly. "I can't prove it on you, Miss Carberry, and I'm too smart to try. But I don't trust you. Come right down to it, practically all the trouble we've had in this building's been up

to you; and that Jamieson woman claims that it was
you, and that you knocked her husband on the head
and made him act as though he had been drinking."

"Then she's a fool," said Tish sharply. "He'd
been drinking."

Which was a fatal slip, for it cost her twenty dollars for a new windowpane and the veterinary's bill
for examining the dog.

But our dear Tish was not daunted. To be safe,
she transferred her practice to the roof and from
there lowered her weights into the alley, usually deserted at night, however, by that fatality which was
to pursue us from first to last of that dreadful excursion, here once more she met with an accident and
as a result we started south a day or two earlier than
we had planned and thus precipitated the real
calamity.

On the evening in question, Tish had raised and
lowered the irons several times without trouble. Being then weary, she rested them on the coping of
the roof, and was surveying the beauties of the night
when she heard certain sounds below. She peered
over, and she saw the janitor of her building stagger-
ing along carrying a heavy box, and accompanied
by a policeman. They were conversing amiably, and
she heard the policeman say:

"Better get in before that old hellcat sees you.
She's a dry, isn't she?"

"Dry?" said the janitor, panting somewhat. "She
makes the Sahara desert look like a fresh-water lake.
She'd think nothing of smashing a case like this."

With that, moving suddenly in the darkness, our

unfortunate Tish must have touched the weights; for they went over and dropped with incredible rapidity, followed by a crash as of glass and a burst of really sickening profanity. She had only time to see the policeman lying in the alley, and to reel in, when she heard the janitor rushing up the stairs, and hammering at her door.

Hannah admitted him, and of course Tish was not there. But in the interval she had had time to lock the door to the roof and from that secure spot to consider the situation.

It was not pleasant. The janitor was on guard at the foot of the stairs, shouting that something had cost sixty-five dollars; and the policeman was sitting up in the alley and feeling around for his helmet. Also at least a dozen cats had discovered the liquor in the alley, and were fighting and love-making in the most shocking manner.

She is a truthful woman, but she says the spectacle of a half dozen domestic and beloved family cats trying under the electric light in the alley to walk dizzily along the top of a fence, and falling off time after time, or caressing one another promiscuously, not only seriously interfered with her train of thought, but was one of the greatest arguments for temperance she had ever witnessed.

"It proved to me conclusively," she has since said, "that liquor first attacks and destroys the higher attributes. Those creatures had no repressions. None!"

But in the end the policeman rose and moved off, although unsteadily, and she was free to consider a method of escape.

By leaning over the coping she was able to tap on Hannah's window with the end of the rod, and having thus engaged her attention, to instruct her to place a folded card table on the top platform of the fire escape, and on that a ladder. This done, and Hannah steadying the ladder, Tish made her descent without difficulty; although she had failed to count on the policeman, who saw her at the last moment and fired a shot at her, fortunately without result.

The rest of the night she spent in packing, and thus it happened that we left for the South a day or so earlier than expected, and without seeing Charlie Sands again. True, we telephoned him at the last moment and he managed to get to the train. But it was already moving, and although he shouted something at us and pointed at the train, we could not hear him.

"I dare say he has left some candy with the conductor," Aggie said. "Candy or fruit. Something nice."

But it was nothing pleasant that Charlie Sands had left, as we were to learn later on.

Just before the train pulled out, a large stout man had got on, in a very bad humor. He was shouting that he had engaged a drawing room, and was going to have it. But he did not secure it, and breathing heavily, he sat down across from us and glared at everybody in the car. He had a seven-foot fishing rod with him, in a canvas cover, and I really believe that our misfortunes began when, on her way to get a drink of water, Tish happened to trip over the end of it.

He was in a rage at once.

"Why don't you watch your feet, madam?" he shouted.

"Why don't you keep that telegraph pole out of the aisle?" said Tish urbanely. "Or hang it out the window and put a flag on it?"

Well, he could not hope to cope with our dear Tish's satiric humor, so he merely uncovered the rod and examined it carefully, and after that he rubbed it with a clean silk handkerchief. As Tish observed, if it had been a baby he could not have handled it more tenderly.

During that first two hours he had quarreled with the porter and the conductor, and glared at Tish in the intervals. And when he had fought with his waiter in the dining car he seemed to feel better, and he came back and unlocked a tin box, divided into compartments. He took out a number of long shiny objects with hooks on, and began to polish those. He tested the points on the hooks, and one he even filed with a small file. And when that was done he took a reel out of a velvet-lined box and oiled and polished it.

I must admit that we were interested, and I had hoped that we might later on enter in conversation with him. But he was placed at our table in the dining car that night, and Aggie, who was sitting in a draft, happened to sneeze and so upset a cup of hot coffee in his lap.

"Good heavens, woman!" he yelled, leaping to his feet. "If you've got to sneeze, why don't you do it in private?"

"If you've got to howl at everybody," Aggie retorted, "why dod't you do that id private? If I had your dispositiod, I'd have sobebody operate od it."

He merely gave us all a long and bitter look and left the dining car. Nor did we see him for some hours that evening, as he had retired to the smoking compartment and remained there. Indeed, it was not until we were all safely in bed that he reappeared, and then a most unfortunate contretemps occurred.

Aggie, who sees badly anyhow, made a mistake that is entirely natural when the berths are made up in a car, and all look alike. She got into the berth opposite me instead of the next one, and had barely crawled under the coverings and put out the light when the Unknown came down the aisle, sat down on her, and was about to remove his shoes, when she rallied sufficiently to protest.

"Get off of me, you wretch!" she said loudly. "How dare you?"

Well, he leaped into the aisle, and really I have never heard a man carry on so. He was no gentleman—I will say that to my dying day, no matter what Charlie Sands may think—for he made our poor Aggie, clad only in her nightdress, move into her own berth, and when he found her menthol inhaler on the window sill he simply flung it out into the aisle.

But all this was nothing to what followed.

I had been asleep for some time, and so had Tish, as I could hear from that heavy breathing which is characteristic of her when completely relaxed, when I heard tense voices in the aisle, punctuated by agitated sneezing.

"How did I know your watch wath there?" Aggie was lisping. "Let go my hand! I tell you—"

"You'll tell a policeman at the next stop!"

"I merely reathed under your pillow—"

"I know damned well you did. And if that isn't my watch in your hand, what is it?"

And then Aggie rose in her dignity and anger.

"I'll tell you what it ith," she said furiously. "It'th my teeth. I lefth them there, and if they feel the way I do I justh wonder they didn't bite you."

Happily our dear Tish slept through all this, and except that Aggie sneezed steadily until almost morning, the rest of the night was peaceful enough.

The next day was comparatively quiet. Only one unpleasantness marred the day. The Monster, as Aggie had named him, spent his time again in the men's compartment at the end of the car, and also rose late, as the porter was trying to get the coffee stains out of his trousers.

This unpleasantness arose out of a natural interest on Tish's part in the tin box.

"He is evidently an experienced fisherman," she said, "and a selfish one. In that box he has various sorts of devices for game fish, but even while polishing them he holds the cloth so we cannot see them. That is not the attitude of a true sportsman, and I resent it."

"Let it alone, Tish," I begged her. "It's locked anyhow, and that man is dangerous."

But she was already feeling for a wire hairpin and

ordering Aggie to stand on watch outside the men's room, and to notify her if the Monster gave signs of leaving it. It was simply bad luck that Aggie chose the wrong end of the car, and stood for one hour and twenty minutes outside the women's lavatory. But she did so, and when the Monster returned Tish had a number of objects from the box in her lap and was carefully examining his reel. She unluckily dropped it when she saw him, and it rolled under a seat.

Well, I thought he was going to have apoplexy. He swore dreadfully, and got down on his knees to hunt the thing. He continued to use the most profane language, and when Tish rose in indignation and the rest of the stuff went on the floor, he simply groaned out loud.

When he had gathered up all the stuff he stood in the aisle and gazed at us, and I must say he looked haggard.

"Would it appeal to your better natures, ladies," he asked, "if I tell you that my doctor has ordered me on a vacation, and that he has specifically mentioned quiet and peace? Peace at meals and plenty of sleep? Because if it does not, I shall be obliged to leave the train."

"A series of unfortunate incidents," Tish replied, "has given you an unfair opinion of us. But you may rest assured that from now on we shall see that you are undisturbed."

He looked almost pleasant at that and sat down, after bowing. But unluckily one of the hooked arrangements had been overlooked in the corner of the seat, and the way he carried on was something terrible. I believe the porter was obliged to cut out the hook, but at least he did not again reappear in the car. The porter came to us later on, grinning, and said he was in the men's room and intended to remain there.

"You ladies certainly did make that genleman suffah," he said, with admiration. "An' you certainly did ruin that pair o' pants foh him. Seems he set considerable store by them. Yes, ma'am, he's certainly suffahed."

I believe the Monster, as we now referred to him, slept somewhere else that night, for we did not see him again. And as by this time we had reached the Southland, our dear Tish relaxed and showed signs of pleasure.

"Observe these islands, Lizzie, scattered along this tropic coast. What bliss to be on one, to have time to think, to commune with the soul. To bathe in the sea, to lie on the sand and receive the actinic rays of the sun, to shake a tree and bring down the necessary food. Lizzie, have you ever thought how little it requires to sustain life?"

"It would take more than you have mentioned to sustain me," I said. "I like a good broiled chop myself now and then. And if you mean those coconuts, how would you propose to get them down?"

But she only eyed me dreamily.

"They train monkeys to do that," she said. "You send one up and then throw stones at him. When he is sufficiently angered he throws down the nuts. I believe the natives grow quite expert at catching them."

"Well, I can't eat coconut," I said. "It gives me indigestion."

That closed the discussion, although I was to recall it later with a certain bitterness.

III

It was a shock to all of us, I think, to find the Monster on the hotel boat, going over to our island; and the way he glared at us was downright wicked. He cheered up, however, when another stout redfaced man on the boat went up to him and struck him heavily on the back.

"Hello, old-timer," he shouted. "Going to get your diamond button this time?"

"That's what I'm here for."

"Bet you a hundred dollars I beat you to it."

"Hell, I hate to work so hard for a hundred dollars. Make it worth while and I'll go you."

It was then that Tish made the remark which so impressed both Aggie and myself. "Where every prospect pleases, and only man is vile."

It is not necessary to relate the details of our arrival and of settling into our cottage. These are unimportant, although while we were registering we all observed that the Monster drew the manager aside and spoke to him at length, while gazing at us. We unpacked, and Aggie put on her foulard while Tish and I wore our black silks to dinner. The Monster was at a table with the other red-faced man, and between them was a very pretty girl who looked sulky and had nothing much to say.

That was our first view of Lily.

After the meal we inspected the tarpon room, and I must say that the size of the stuffed fish rather worried me. Also there were photographs of the fish fighting, and they looked dangerous in the extreme. Aggie turned a little pale, especially as there were other photographs of alligators, sharks, devilfish, and even of an octopus or two.

The girl wandered in about that time and lit a cigarette, and Tish addressed her.

"I perceive that the king of fish is the main pursuit of this resort," she said.

"I'll say it is," said the girl rather shortly.

"It must indeed be a royal sport."

"It's not a sport; it's a mania," she said. "It doesn't matter what you've got in your head; what you've got on a hook is all that counts."

And with that she turned and went out again.

Aggie and I knitted that evening, while Tish saw to the boat. The Monster was playing poker, and the girl wandered about until he was settled and then with a tall good-looking man disappeared outside. Aggie watched them go, for the blighting of her own early romance—she was at one time engaged to a Mr. Wiggins, who was in the roofing business, and slipped on a rainy day—has left her with a soft spot for all lovers.

"It is an ideal spot for affairs of the heart, Lizzie," she said. "Yet those two are not happy."

"Maybe he didn't get a fish today," I said sharply. For all the conversation I could hear was about fish and fishing.

But Aggie is strongly intuitive, and later events were to prove her right. If the time was to come when we wished that we had never seen Lily, there was nothing to warn us then or for several days to come.

For a day or so nothing happened. We had packed our case of provisions and bottled water in the boat, as the tarpon were not yet in, and were making preliminary excursions to study the channels and passes. Our bathing suits, skirts, and large sun hats made these excursions comfortable. Also it was during these more or less idle hours that we practiced our life belt drill. The belts were laid in a row in the boat; on Tish's count of "one" we stooped, "two," we picked them up, and at "three" we adjusted them.

As it developed, this drill was to save our poor Aggie's life later on.

But Aggie was growing increasingly nervous. One day we returned to find a large shark lying on the pier, and she could hardly be induced to pass it.

"They eat people, Tish!" she cried.

"Only when driven by extreme hunger, Aggie," Tish told her patiently.

"How do you know when they're hungry?" she demanded "I don't suppose they go around pointing down their throats."

Tish's enthusiasm was unabated, however, and she continued to prepare for the day when the tarpon would come in from the cool depths of the Gulf.

She had purchased a length of rope, and it was to be my duty, once the fish had struck, to lash her to her chair, which in turn was screwed to the deck of the boat. At the same time Aggie was to fill and hold ready a pail of water, in case the reel became heated and began to smoke.

We saw little of the Monster, although now and then we could hear him shouting at the waitress in the dining room. It appeared that by that time he and the other red-faced man had wagered a thousand dollars on a diamond-button fish, and they spent most of the time scouting around outside the passes looking for tarpon. They were out day and night, and all the hotel people could talk about was the bet between them.

And then, on a day when the wind prohibited fishing, we had a brief talk with Lily.

We had taken our knitting to the beach, and I remember that the sand was covered with small fiddler crabs, all running sideways and very annoying, and that Aggie immediately returned to our cottage and brought back an insect spray which was intended for mosquitoes. By thoroughly spraying a portion of the sand we cleared a place on which to sit, and hardly had Tish lain down with her face to the sun than we all heard a sound of muffled sobbing.

It came from some palm trees, and we discovered that it was Lily, face down and crying bitterly.

With her customary kindness Tish moved over and sat down beside her.

"I perceive," she said, "that you are unhappy. Yet in this lovely spot—"

"Oh, go away," said the girl, without looking up. "If I want to cry, that's my affair."

"In a week," said Tish, "you will wonder why you have wept."

"Will I?" said Lily rudely, and suddenly sat up. "What do you know about it? I've had this for twenty years. Don't come around here and tell me—"

"Had what?" Tish inquired gently.

"Father," said Lily. "And the way I feel about him is nobody's business. I'll tell you this: I've been hoping all morning that he'd go in bathing. There's a shark out there."

Tish glanced at Aggie and myself.

"I think I know him."

"Well, you'll have heard him anyhow," said Lily. "A red-faced man, and inclined to be violent?"

"Inclined to be! Listen! Last year his boatman fell over his rod and broke it, just as a tarpon struck, and he threw the man overboard."

As she began to weep again at this moment, Aggie, who is the soul of kindness, brought her some blackberry cordial. She took it suspiciously, but in a few minutes she was feeling better.

"That's great stuff," she said. "If I had a feather in my hand, I could fly."

But she confided no more to us, although she was much more cheerful and even did a dance step or two on the beach before she departed.

"If you see a handsome youth looking for me,"

she called back, "give him some of that medicine of yours and send him in to bite father!"

Tish was very thoughtful. It was clear to her, she said, that the young man was mixed up in Lily's trouble, and that the Monster was more than usually unpleasant because of the wager; that if he got a diamond-button fish before the other man he would be more reasonable, and that it was clearly our duty to help him get such a fish.

"Like the man or not," she observed, "the happiness of two young hearts lies in his keeping. And if we can in any way assist him to such a fish, it becomes our duty to do so."

Both Aggie and I perceived the nobility of the idea, and I wish to say now that in all that followed, unfortunate as it was, this was Tish's ruling thought.

Nevertheless, with that fatality which pursued us throughout, that very evening we were unwittingly to rouse his suspicion against us once more.

The late afternoon boat brought Tish a telegram from Charlie Sands:

WIRES FROM CERTAIN PERSON INDICATE
BAD FISHING AND EQUAL BAD HUMOR.
TRUSTING YOU TO DO YOUR BIT AS AGREED.

But as it was then dinnertime, and we were to practice with our rods and reels that night from a small bridge which led from the golf links to a pavilion on our islet, Tish put it in her knitting bag and quite forgot it. And the events of that night put it out of her head entirely.

Briefly, on the bridge all had gone well that evening until we heard a boat rapidly approaching and about to pass under it. Both Tish and I reeled in, but Aggie unluckily had twisted her line and was unable to do so. Just what occurred I do not know, but the next moment the boat had hurled itself at the island with a terrific crash and climbed almost to the pavilion.

In the really dreadful silence that followed I could hear Tish whispering to us to run; this we did, although as the end of her rod had struck Aggie in the chest she could go neither fast nor far. In the end we found safety in a sand trap on the links and lay there for some hours. Most uncomfortably, as the sand immediately irritated Aggie's nose and started her to sneezing, and as we were extremely anxious about Tish.

We had heard her running rapidly toward the hotel, and a moment or so later the Monster and his boatman followed. But Tish carries no surplus weight as I do, and we learned from her later that she was well in the lead from the start.

"I had sufficient time," she said, "to leave my rod on the back veranda, go inside, and pick up my knitting. But I think he suspects me, Lizzie. He stood outside a window and shook his fist at me."

Well, it really was unfortunate, because the tarpon came in that night for a short time, and the other man brought in a fish only a pound and a half under the diamond-button weight. But Lily's father went down to the pier to look at it, and then insisted on having it cut open. The other man objected, but it was finally done, and they found that three eight-ounce weights had been rammed down its throat.

The other man claimed that his boatman must have done it while his back was turned, because he had promised him a hundred dollars if the fish made the weight. But there was a great deal of hard feeling all around, and it was agreed that both men would go out without boatmen thereafter. All of which has a bearing on this narrative, whether Charlie Sands thinks so or not. Because if the Monster had had a boatman along on that terrible night later, things might have been different.

The tarpon had disappeared again, and the wind was still high. All the fishermen were in an unchristion frame of mind, but the Monster was really dreadful. Even golf did not soothe him, and one day when we were watching and Aggie happened to sneeze just as he drove off at the last hole, he sent his ball into the water and turned on us in a frenzy of rage.

"Great suffering snakes!" he yelled. "Can't you women keep away from me? That's all I ask: just keep away. And if this island isn't big enough, find another island. Any island!"

Well, later on we did exactly that and he did not like it. He was certainly a difficult person, and when Lily's young man won the golf match that day he walked right up to Aggie and accused her of sneezing on purpose.

"It's persecution!" he yelled. "That's what it is. What did I ever do to you women anyhow?"

Then he broke the golf club he had in his hand and stalked away.

It was that night that Tish had another telegram from Charlie Sands.

ARE YOU MIXED UP IN SITUATION IN ANY MANNER? PLEASE REPLY.

But, as our dear Tish said with dignity, it did not deserve any reply, and so she sent none.

Looking back over that situation, I can see how one more event led up to the catastrophe, and by eliciting Tish's interest in the young man himself, finally precipitated the crisis.

IV

This event was our meeting with Lily's young man himself, on the pier one night.

We had thought we were alone until we perceived a pair of white flannel trousers lying prone on the flooring.

"Dear me," Tish said, peering at them. "What a strange place for a pair of trousers!"

And then a muffled voice spoke, from over the edge of the pier.

"I'm in them," it said, "and if I ever get this —— —— hook out from under this —— —— edge—"

"I don't like your language," Tish said severely.

"Then you'd better go away," said the voice. "The

way things are, I may swear for an hour, or possibly two."

And then he overreached himself and fell right over the edge and into the water.

He came to the surface in a moment or so, however, and holding onto a piling, with his head above the water, he inspected us.

"Sorry," he said. "I thought you were three other fellows. Well, I'm calmer now. Nothing like a cold bath to restore the good old morale. Why struggle? Why suffer?"

"You sound unhappy," said Tish.

"Unhappy? That's a mild word, ladies. I'm as unhappy as hell. When I consider that by merely ducking my head under this surface for a sufficient length of time I should cease to suffer, I am tempted, strongly tempted."

And with that he suddenly disappeared into the sea. Never shall I forget my agony of mind, or Aggie's hysterical moaning.

"He has done it," she cried. "He has ended it all." And she sneezed violently.

In a moment, to our great relief, he reappeared at the steps of the pier and pulled himself out of the water. He was quite calm, but he inspected himself ruefully.

"You can see," he said, "that luck is against me. As I said, why struggle? Why suffer? These are my best flannel trousers, and they are shrinking as I speak. Also, I have learned finally and forever that I shall never make a fisherman. There was a faint hope, but it is gone. I've had that infernal hook everywhere, from the back of my neck to underneath the dock, where it is now; everywhere except in a fish's mouth."

Well, as he was thoroughly wet and also despondent, Tish sent Aggie at once for some blackberry cordial, and it gave him a more cheerful outlook on life. He declined to go to the hotel and change his clothing, but said that he felt like talking.

"I feel," he said, "the urge to tell the story of my life, if you will bear with me, and if someone will watch that bottle and see that it does not fall into the sea. The thought of all the little fishes going gaga and—but never mind about that.

"I was born," he went on, "with a complex against fishing. It is an early impression, rather, due to seeing my nurse eat fish for forty days in Lent. However that may be, I loathe and despise fishing. From the squirming of the worm to the squirming of the unlucky fish, it is horrible to me.

"Judge then of my tragedy when I find the one, the only, girl and discover not only that her father is a fisherman, but that he is a fanatic on the subject. Where other men celebrate a winning in the stock market with wine, he goes out and buys a new reel; he inspects his lines with a magnifying glass; his house is full of stuffed fish mounted on boards. He measures a man by the line he can put out on a cast; his idea of a kiss is the way a trout fly falls onto the water. Just why his daughter wasn't born with scales—"

"That will do," said Tish sternly.

"Well, you've got the idea. He's here, and it's all

off. He wants a son-in-law only to take fishing, and I came here, so to speak, on trial. But I went asleep the first day he took me out in a boat; I lost his best reel for him; and I loosened a front tooth for him one day practicing a back cast. And now he's made a fool wager on a diamond-button fish, and I'm only excess baggage."

He was silent for a moment.

"What I ought to do," he said moodily, "is to go home and forget it. And her. I'm doing no good here. I can't even eat. The way her father looks at me in the dining room gives me indigestion. I've got it now. Perhaps a little more of that cordial would help it."

He cheered after he had taken a glass, and said that he had had various ideas. One of them was to bore a hole in the old man's boat, and watch him slowly sink. Another was to drain out his gasoline, all but a little, and let him drift to sea, slowly dying of hunger and thirst.

"But the really big idea," he observed, "would be to land him all alone on one of those empty islands, and let nature take its course!"

Yes, I admit that he said that. But for him to have told Charlie Sands later on that the island was his idea was really absurd. As Charlie Sands must realize now, the island was purely an accident.

On the way back to the cottage Tish commented on his recital.

"All in all," she said, "this young man would be better off out of that family. Nevertheless, our duty is plain. If the Monster, as Aggie calls him, is to be placated by winning this wager, we must be near at hand to help him in emergency."

And again I repeat that this was Tish's kindly idea from the start. She is ever friendly to young love, and to lovers; and in spite of his attitude toward us, she bore no malice toward the man who was later to place us in so awkward a position.

And now I come with a certain reluctance to the further events of that night, which made for a time such a diametric change in our habits of living; forcing on us indeed the need to shift for ourselves under most unpropitious conditions.

As we passed the hotel on our way to the cottage we saw a man run out in fishing garb, followed by others, and we realized that at last the tarpon had reached the passes in numbers. We at once shifted into our bathing suits with the skirts over them, and in our haste neglected to take our mackintoshes or other wraps; an oversight which we were bitterly to regret, especially Aggie.

It was Tish's idea that we follow the Monster's boat and this we did, although to our surprise he did not go in the usual direction, but headed down the coast.

"Many fishermen," Tish informed us, "have secret places of their own, and use them only when safe from observation. We will follow him."

I think he must have heard our engine, for he speeded up and went very fast; but we also moved rapidly and kept close behind him. It was indeed an eerie feeling, following the sound of his engine through the darkness; once we went aground on a

mud bank, and it was necessary for all of us to remove our clothing and work the boat off. As the
night was cold, it was a trying business, and it was
at that time that our poor Aggie stepped onto a large
crab, which closed on one of her toes and held on.
A most painful matter.

But we soon located him again, and finally came
to a stop not far from his boat. We knew nothing of
our surroundings, or even where we were. But there
was no time to worry. All the water about us was
filled with the great creatures; they swam and rolled
and leaped, and suddenly Tish shouted that she had
one, and a colossal body shot out of the darkness and
hit the water with a thud.

I shall omit the details of that struggle. We at once
put on our life belts, and soon it became necessary
to lash our valiant Tish to her chair, which was fortunately screwed to the deck. All the time the creature was leaping. It was then that I noticed that our
boat was drawing near the other, and that the Monster was shouting at us.

"Keep off me," he shouted. "Start your engine,
you idiots! I've got a fish on!"

But as we were still some distance away, and also
fully occupied, we paid no attention. Our dear Tish
was having all she could do to hold on to her rod,
although she managed to gasp that both her shoulders were dislocated, and I was standing by to render
assistance if necessary, when a terrible and unexpected thing happened.

In the faint starlight we heard a hideous tearing
and smashing of wood, and the other boat rose in

the air and then settled back again. We realized with horror what had occurred: Tish's fish had risen like a projectile under his boat and had practically wrecked it.

There was a really dreadful silence, followed by the Monster's voice.

"You —— —— idiots!" he yelled. "You've torn the bottom out of my boat!"

"Nonsense!" Tish called angrily. "The fish did it. If he chooses to try to drown you he's only doing what a lot of people have contemplated anyhow."

"Get over here, I tell you! This boat's sinking under me."

But I had just started the engine when a really terrible thing happened. The tarpon jumped into our boat.

Never shall I forget that moment. It was an enormous creature, and as it leaped about in the darkness one could hear the furniture smashing. Almost at once I heard a chair go overboard, and as I crawled up onto the roof of the cabin I heard a shout from Aggie, followed by a dull splash, and realized that our poor friend had followed the chair and was afloat in her life belt on that vast expanse of water.

"Aggie!" I called in anguish. "Aggie, where are you?"

Although I could hear her coughing and sneezing somewhere out in that vast expanse, she said nothing; we were now moving rapidly, and the sounds grew more and more faint. All that could be heard was the voice of the Monster, shouting that he was sinking, and an occasional grunt from Tish as the fish struck her a resounding blow.

She was struggling to untie herself, but the knot was at the back of the chair.

It was a terrible situation, with the fish in complete control of the boat, and with one thing following another into the sea: the box of canned foods on which we depended in emergency, the barrel in which we placed our smaller fish, one after another went flying overboard.

And then Tish spoke.

"If you could catch it around the middle you might get rid of it, Lizzie. We really should go back for Aggie."

"Catch it!" I said, from the roof of the cabin. "It doesn't stay long enough in one place for me to see it."

"You could stun it with something."

"It didn't stun it perceptibly to go through the bottom of a boat," I said bitterly. "Well, you've got your fish. You've learned something about the depths of the sea, and what are you going to do about it?"

All this had taken some little time, but at that moment the fish took another jump and went overboard, and I was enabled to untie Tish. She at once took charge, but what was our horror to find that the miserable creature had broken the tiller rope, and that our boat was completely unmanageable! Also, we had no idea where we were. It was in vain that Tish stopped the engine and called into the darkness. There was no sound whatever from Aggie, and to make matters worse the night was now inky black.

It was indeed a tragic situation, and to add to our anxiety our gasoline was running low. We spoke in low voices of our poor Aggie drifting hither and yon at the mercy of the tides, and Tish, a kindly soul, even spoke well of the Monster.

"He was the victim of an obsession, Lizzie," she said. "And of course it is possible that he could swim. In that case—"

It was a dreary night, nor did dawn reveal a cheerful prospect. The tide had carried us far into the Gulf, and it was her fear that it had done the same thing with Aggie.

"Bottles placed in the Gulf Stream down here," she said, "are frequently picked up along the shores of Newfoundland."

At last we saw land to the east, a number of islands, and were able with the last of our gasoline to reach one of them. Never can I depict the depression of that landing, or of the thought that years later our dear comrade might be washed ashore on some forsaken spot along the Atlantic coast.

But it is not like Tish to despair, and finding that we had one rod remaining, she at once set about fishing for our breakfast, using the fiddler crabs which covered the beach. She had just brought in a fair-sized sheepshead—a very succulent fish—and I was building a fire, when we heard violent sneezing down the beach and looked up to see Aggie, alive and in the flesh, gazing toward us. She was still wearing her life belt, and as she approached we saw that her usual friendly manner had changed.

"Aggie!" I said. "How did you get here?"

"I just drifted id," she said. "And do thaks to either ob you. To throw be overboard ad thed abadod be. I did'dt thik it of either of you."

Tish had been eying her.

"Nobody abandoned you," she said. "But you *look* abandoned, all right. Where's your skirt?"

And it was then that Aggie burst into tears.

"A shark took it," she said, and collapsed onto the beach.

Well, she had really had a difficult time and had taken a bad cold into the bargain. She had floated around for some time, but she had got her chest full of water and couldn't call out. She heard the Monster swearing frightfully, and at last she heard him swimming, but then everything was quiet. The tarpon bothered her considerably, she said, because they took to jumping all around her and rather knocking her about. But she was really all right until some large fish, she thought a shark, took hold of her skirt and made off with it.

They had gone quite a distance before she managed to unfasten her skirt, but after that things were simpler. She found she was close to land, and at dawn she had succeeded, by using her arms as oars, in rowing herself in.

"But I wadt sobe tea," she said tearfully. "Sobe hot tea ad toast ad a boiled egg, Tish. I'be cold, ad I'be puckered. Look at be."

And this was true. Owing to her long immersion in the water her skin was in a wrinkled condition, like a laundress' hands.

I began at once to fry the fish, for luckily our cooking implements, some sugar, salt and pepper and a jar of salad dressing, had been in the cabin and been saved. But it was sad to watch Aggie when we admitted that we had no gasoline, and were marooned on the island for an indefinite period. Sadder still to admit that our food was gone, and that there were no eggs and no tea.

"Of all the idiotic thigs!" she said angrily. "You might have *sat* od the food box, Lizzie. If I'be to be drowed all dight ad starved all day—"

Then she stopped and stared up the beach.

"It's hib!" she said. "The Bodster!" And as she was practically unclothed she had merely time to cover her lower limbs with sand before he was on us.

He was in a towering rage, and he looked very queer. He had no coat and no shoes, and his necktie was hanging in a wet string around his neck. He was shouting at us long before he reached us, and he fixed on Tish at once.

"You—you menace!" he bellowed. "Look at me! Look at your work. I've lost my watch. I've lost my coat. I've lost my pipe and my tobacco. I've lost my boat and my fish and a thousand dollars on a bet; and I've d——d near lost my life. Killing's too good for you. Torture! Torture's what you need."

He stopped there for breath, and suddenly he saw the fish frying on the fire. That seemed to incense him still further.

"I'll have you jailed," he said in a choking voice. "You can all go to jail and rot. You not only leave me to drown; you come here and have a picnic on the strength of it. Well, go on and picnic! I'm going home."

And with that he waded out into the water and crawled into the boat.

"Now see how you like it," he shouted. "Maybe I'll send back for you someday, and maybe I won't. Probably not. I've got a bad memory."

And with that he tried to start the engine.

He worked over it for twenty minutes, without result, but Tish merely ignored him. We were already eating our frugal breakfast when at last he came ashore. He had the good taste to pass us by and go on, but he took a good look at the food, and I am certain that he hesitated.

"You'll hear from me later," he said, and disappeared along the beach.

We were all more cheerful after we had eaten, and Tish pointed out the advantages of our position.

"We have a case of bottled water," she said, "and if Charlie Sands is correct, there should be plenty of eggs buried along the shore. Also, as we shall need a balanced ration, the heart of a palm tree will provide an excellent salad, for which we have the dressing already prepared. Also we possess an ax to cut down the tree. Sorry as I am to destroy any tree, in this case the end must justify the means. We shall also have coconuts, as I observe a number of them over our heads."

"Exactly," said Aggie. "Over our heads. If you

thik I'b goig to clibe ode of those trees, Tish Carberry—"

Tish eyed the tree in question thoroughly.

"With coconut milk and eggs, we could have custard," she said. "There is sugar on the boat, and a
bottle of vanilla extract. And if I am not mistaken,
there is an oyster bar out there. Oysters, fish, salad,
and dessert—no, we shall not starve, Aggie."

The breakfast had heartened all of us, and as the
warm sun came out even Aggie looked less puckered.
But she missed her skirt horribly, and as she was
threatened with severe sunburn, spent most of the
morning in the water once more, standing there
rather pathetically, waist-deep. It was not possible
to seek shelter in the interior of the island, as we had
early discovered that everything in it jagged, including the grass.

Later in the morning Tish and I made a tour of
the island, Tish looking for various food possibilities and I watching for a boat that might rescue us.
This last was but a faint hope, and it faded when at
last, seeing a fishing boat, I waved wildly to it and
the fisherman merely waved back cheerfully.

Curiously enough, we saw nothing of the Monster. But this was explained when on our return we
found no sign whatever of Aggie, and that the
Monster was seated by the remains of our fire, with
his head in his hands.

"Great heavens!" Tish gasped. "He's done away
with her."

But his expression as we approached was far from
bloodthirsty. He looked up at us, and he was as de-

jected and sorry an object as I have ever laid eyes on.

"Look here," he said hollowly. "Maybe I've been a little hasty. Anyhow, you people have got to give me some decent water. You've got some locked up in that boat."

"There's water on the island," Tish said coldly.

"That pond's full of wigglers, madam."

"Then strain it."

"Strain it? With what? I haven't even got a handkerchief. Am I to strain it through the seat of my trousers?"

"You needn't be vulgar," Tish reproved him. "For that matter, a few wigglers won't hurt you. And now I'll ask you to move on. We are only three weak women. You will have to shift for yourself."

"Shift for myself! Who brought me to this?" he said furiously. "And three weak women! Good God, madam, if you'd been any weaker I'd not be alive this minute. I warn you, I'm desperate. I'm not safe. I need food and water, and I'm ready to break open that boat to get them."

"Give him the keys, Lizzie. You will find there," she said to him, "some sugar, salt and pepper, salad dressing, and vanilla extract."

"Vanilla extract!" he groaned. "Yes, you'd be sure to have vanilla extract! What the devil am I to do with vanilla extract? I tell you, I need food."

But Tish merely observed that the island was full of food and that he would better move on. We were about to get dinner. He stared at us queerly and got up.

"Very well," he said. "I'll move on, all right. I'll

feel safer alone. There's an alligator on the other side of the island, and I'd rather have him for company anyhow."

Before he left he asked humbly enough for a few matches.

"For what?" Tish demanded.

"To light a fire, madam. A fire's cheerful. James and I would enjoy a fire. James is the alligator. For warmth only, of course. *We* have nothing to cook."

'All this had taken some time, and when he had gone our poor Aggie emerged from the undergrowth as if she had been fired out of a gun. She said she had at last found a tree trunk to sit on, and being weary after her night's exertion, had dozed lightly. When she wakened a large rattlesnake was sleeping on the tree trunk beside her, and for some time she had not dared to move.

She was quite tremulous, and while Tish and I prepared our midday meal she interred herself once more in the sand and was fairly comfortable, although she complained that a number of small fiddler crabs, appreciating the warmth of her body, were cuddling against her.

Luncheon, always a light meal with us, consisted largely of the delicious stone crabs which were buried along a certain mangrove bank. These Tish brought in, and when boiled and cooled the claws with a French dressing made a delightful meal, and afterward Tish and I left the camp to find if possible a coconut or two on the ground.

We were gone for some hours, and I blame ourselves rather than Aggie for what happened. As we have repeatedly explained to Charlie Sands, Aggie's situation was desperate. Not only did she feel indecent, but what with mosquitoes and sunburn her lower limbs were in a highly painful condition. As a matter of fact, the Monster was left in no worse condition than hers had been.

It happened as follows:

Tish and I were returning, when we saw a strange figure on the beach. It was not the Monster, being much shorter, but it wore trousers, and Tish at once said that we were saved.

"They have found us, Lizzie," she said. "There is a boy, coming to get us."

But I was not so certain. There was something familiar about the walk, and in truth it turned out to be Aggie, clad in the Monster's trousers.

"Aggie!" Tish said sternly. "If you have made friends with that Monster, that wretch, that unspeakable individual, then—"

But Aggie, who had been sneezing violently with excitement, shook her head.

"Hardly freds, Tish," she said. "He's too far out to hear much, but sobe of the thigs he's called be are terrible."

"Out where?"

"Od the oyster bar."

Well, it appears that hardly had we started than the Monster appeared again, and Aggie had to retire into the bushes. This time, however, she escaped snakes by climbing a tree, and from there she saw all that happened.

The Monster dug around our ashes and finding the shells of the claws, began to examine them feverishly. But he found nothing, and he then sat down and stared fixedly out to sea. After a time he apparently noticed the oyster bar, and in a moment and to her consternation he was taking off his trousers. Clad thus, in his fishing shirt and underwear, he at once waded out to the bar, and began to detach oysters and breaking them open, to eat them in great numbers. Now and then he looked back at the beach, but as he saw no one he must have felt safe.

But Aggie was struggling against temptation. There on the sand in full view lay protection for her lower limbs, lay warmth at night and decency by day; and at last she succumbed.

Tish was thoughtful during this recital.

"I see no objection," she said at last, "to an equal distribution; to a day-about arrangement, for example. You have them one day and he the next. If he has any sense of fairness whatever he will agree. After all, you are a woman. Where is he?"

"He's still od the bar, ad the tide is cobig id."

This proved to be accurate. Indeed, when after spending some time looking for a palm tree which would be available for salad, we reached our camp again, only his head was above water. But he could still speak. Never in my life, before or since, have I heard such language. Aggie stood with her hands in his pockets, and gazed out at him.

"He cad swib," she said. "It's only false pride,

Tish. He'd let be go about exposed id a bathig suit, but he's too proud to be seed id his shirt. He's got udderwear too, which I hadd't."

Well, the tide was still coming in, and finally he did swim to shore, landing at some distance away on a point. There he stood for some time, shaking his fists at us and apparently jumping up and down; but at last he turned and went away, and we were left to peace and a beautiful sunset.

With the coconut milk and some turtle eggs which we found buried in the sand I was able to prepare a very fair omelet for dinner, serving it in the large shells which were scattered over the beach; and as Tish had managed to cut down a young palm, Aggie chilled a salad dressing for it in the sea. Also by grating the coconut into some of its own milk we had a truly delicious drink. Thus fed and comfortable, we slept very well.

But as I have said, coconut gives me indigestion, and toward daybreak it roused me. The night had turned cold, and there was quite a wind. I sat up, and in the starlight I saw a strange and desperate figure. It was bending over Aggie!

With a shriek I roused the others, and the figure quickly departed. We felt, however, that it was not fair to Aggie to sleep again, and we kept watch until morning.

The next two days passed without incident. Our diet, although monotonous, was plentiful, and was varied by a school of mackerel which came in close to shore. With her usual consideration, however,

Tish insisted that we leave the beach each afternoon, to allow the Monster to reach the oyster bar, and also was careful to leave the salt and pepper where he could see them.

It was on the third day, I believe, that he seemed to tire of the oysters. Returning a little earlier than usual, we were in time to see him reach the bar and stand there for some time, looking down at the oysters. He seemed to shake his head in a melancholy manner, and then he turned and waded back without touching any of them.

Tish, observing him narrowly, commented on the fact that this process was carred through in silence.

"He is growing gentler," she observed. "He no longer leaps and shouts. In a few hours he will be open to negotiations."

The nature of the negotiations she did not divulge, but I desire to call attention to the shrewdness of that prophecy. It was indeed but a few hours; at the time of our evening meal, in fact.

We were eating an excellent supper at the time, and his voice, when it came, showed that he was sheltered in underbrush behind us.

"Ladies," he said, "things being as they are, I must ask you not to look around. But I have come to appeal to your better natures. I shall not mention the affair of my trousers. It is a delicate matter. But I have come to speak of food. I find that I am surfeited, fed up, with oysters. Today it was all I could do to face that bar. Once I was fond of oysters, but that is gone. Gone forever."

He seemed to shudder, and Aggie looked at me pitifully. She is very sympathetic. But Tish was uncompromising.

"Lizzie, I'll have a little more of the boiled mackerel," she said, and proceeded to eat it calmly.

"It's like this," he went on in a plaintive voice. "I apologize for everything. Only don't ask me to face that oyster bar again."

"It's your stomach that speaks, not your heart," said Tish firmly.

He seemed to be surprised at that.

"My heart?" he inquired. "What's my heart got to do with it? You don't expect me to be sorry for those d——d oysters, do you?"

And then Tish told him certain uncomplimentary truths.

"You've been a violent man all your life, probably," she said. "A nuisance and a pest. It is likely that you have had money, and that your employees cringe when they confront you. Aggie, I'll have the salad now, please. Yes, undoubtedly they hate you as well as fear you. And you're a bully; your own daughter—"

"What do *you* know about my daughter?" he asked in amazement.

"Enough. I know that she is in love, and that you have thwarted that love. Your conduct has indeed been brutal. She is brokenhearted."

He was silent for a moment or so, and I remember now that he seemed almost too astonished to speak.

"In love?" he said at last. "Are you sure of that?"

"She has told me so."

"Curious," he observed. "I didn't know you knew her. I thought the young man—but never mind about that. I don't suppose you intend to starve me to death as well as steal my pants because my daughter's in love?"

"We might make a reasonable arrangement," Tish told him, "while the dessert is being brought on."

He groaned, and I could fairly feel his eyes boring into me as I carried a caramel custard from the fire.

"Is that a custard?" he asked.

"Yes."

"A caramel custard?"

"It is," Tish told him.

He sighed deeply.

"I used to be fond of caramel custard," he said. "Very fond. It was my favorite dessert. But that was years ago, before I was cast away on an island with three—"

"Three what?" Tish demanded.

"Never mind about that," he said hastily. "You mentioned an arrangement. What is it? I'm only a weak man, and I dare say I'll sell my immortal soul, let alone my daughter, for a square meal. For a square meal and my trousers," he added.

But here Aggie wailed, and Tish firmly stated that the trousers were not to be bargained about. She demanded, and he finally agreed, that he consent to his daughter's engagement, and that he abide by this agreement.

"Go back, send for the man, and give your daughter to him," she said. "That agreement finally drawn and placed in Miss Aggie's pocket—"

"My pocket," he interrupted.

"—we shall be able to discuss rates for board. Lodging unfortunately we cannot offer."

"Rates! You're going to *charge* me?"

"Why not?" said Tish placidly. "I have certain charities, and the funds shall go to them. Breakfast and lunch will be twenty-five dollars, and dinner fifty. If that is all right with you, you can stand behind that tree and we will pass your dinner to you now. There is plenty here."

Well, he carried on dreadfully, far worse than about his daughter; but in the end he agreed, and while Tish was writing the agreement I prepared his meal. I made a tray out of the engine hatch cover, and was about to carry it to him when Tish interfered.

"Payment in advance," she said. "Aggie, take fifty dollars off the roll of bills in your pocket—"

"My pocket," he said again.

"—and give them to me. All right, Lizzie."

I never knew a man to eat so much, and strangely enough, when he had finished we heard him laughing. He sat back there in the darkness and laughed and laughed, and I must say it made me creepy.

"Ladies," he said, "I bow to you. Were conditions other than they are, I would emerge and kneel to you. For sheer highhanded banditry you have the

world beaten by a mile, and as for cooking—!
You've robbed me of my daughter, of my money,
and of my pants—and by gad I'm for you. If any
of you ever want a newspaper job, come to me."

And even then we did not realize the awful truth!
Not even when we were rescued the next day, nor
when within twenty-four hours we received a telegram from Charlie Sands calling Tish home at
once.

FOR GOSH SAKE COME HOME AND EXPLAIN
WIRE FROM BOSS STOP SITUATION TERRIBLE
STOP DON'T WANT THE GIRL AND NEVER DID
STOP WHAT HAS HAPPENED?

We had spent the intervening time in bed and had
seen no one, and now we packed hastily and prepared to go immediately. None of us was surprised
to see Lily and her young man at the dock, and as
he had his arm around her we knew that everything
was as we had planned. But we were a little surprised at a few words which passed between Tish
and Lily just before the boat started.

"Did you hear the news?" she said. "Everything's all right."

Tish smiled at her benignly.

"I am very glad," she said. "We had to use a little
moral suasion, but it has worked out perfectly."

Lily looked a trifle bewildered.

"Really?" she said. "I thought it was because he
had caught a diamond-button tarpon."

Then the boat moved out, and we were left to

consider Charlie Sands' telegram. We could make
nothing of it, however, nor of Charlie Sands' wild
expression when we got out of the train.

"Quick!" he said. "Out with it! What in the name
of gosh-amighty have you done to me?"

"Don't be an idiot," said Tish. "What could we
have done to you?"

Well, he looked fairly stupefied.

"You're sure of that, are you? You don't know
anything and you didn't do anything?"

"We have done a number of things, but none that
concern you or your affairs."

"And you didn't see the boss?"

"Certainly not."

Well, he seemed stunned. He drew a telegram out
of his pocket and handed it to us. It said:

> CERTAINLY YOU MAY HAVE HER MY BOY
> STOP HAD NO IDEA THAT IT WAS SO SERIOUS
> STOP GOOD LUCK TO YOU.

"I've wired back for a confirmation," he said dejectedly, "but it's 'her,' not 'it.' He doesn't mean the
job; he means Clara."

"Tish!" said Aggie suddenly. "You don't suppose—"

But Tish silenced her with a look, and we went
into the station.

I have related this series of incidents as they occurred, and in the hope that Charlie Sands will read
them without bias. He has never been really fair to
us, although after all Clara eloped with somebody

else a few days later. But he did not get the job, and he has always for some reason held it against us. Especially Aggie.

"A woman who will steal a man's only pair of trousers will do anything."

Also it appears that just as soon as Clara had eloped he sent the boss a keg of very fine oysters, and that when they were opened in his presence he turned pale and ordered them out of the office.

"I don't know why," he says. "He used to like oysters. But that very day he gave another chap the job."

But he also says that he is much changed, and that he has ordered that every man on the staff buy two pairs of trousers with every suit. It has become a sort of mania with him.

"A man without trousers is worse than a woman without virtue," he told them. "For one is wicked, but the other is ridiculous."

But he has never told the story, nor have we until now, and that without using his name. As a matter of fact, he asked us not to do so, and that in the following manner:

Although we have not related this to Charlie Sands, the "boss" sent Tish that very keg of oysters, and with it a card.

"The oyster has a mouth, but does not talk."

THE DIPPER

THE DIPPER

I

ONLY LAST night I was looking at the sky, and
the sight of the Dipper brought back to me
forcibly the events of last summer. I went to my
desk, and there I got out the one or two small objects which I had retained as reminders of the
affair: a small piece of black cloth cut, as we later
discovered, from one of the extra curtains of Tish's
car and having two small round holes in it, the notes
made on the third, fourth, and fifth of August, a
box of marshmallows now dried and hard, and a
pair of long spurs which we found discarded by the
cabin when all was over.

So tonight, while Tish is at prayer meeting and
Aggie has retired to her couch, I propose to make
a permanent record of the experience in the hope
that, given chronologically, Charlie Sands will see
that no Christian woman, such as his dear aunt Tish
undoubtedly is, could have done otherwise than as
she did.

As a matter of fact, a portion of the responsibility is actually his. It was he who on her birthday in
the spring presented Tish with the book on the art
of fishing which was the beginning of it all.

"Stream fishing, my beloved aunt," he said, with

emphasis. "Nice quiet creeks and rivers. It may seem a trifle flat after a certain affair which I recall, but the idea is that you catch the fish and not vice versa."

By this he referred to the summer before, when we had rented a cottage on the Maine coast and were wont to take a boat and do a little quiet fishing for codfish, tying our lines to the seats and knitting or reading until a certain agitation showed that something was on the hook.

Unfortunately, on the day in question, our anchor had caught in the blow hole of a whale and for some time it looked as though we were bound for the mid-Atlantic, if not for the British Isles. I remember our passing through a fishing fleet at a terrific pace and that one man called to us to let go.

"If you do get him what'll you do with him?" he said.

I forget our dear Tish's reply, but I do know that we finally collided with a large revenue boat and that, while it freed us, a sailor leaned over the edge and accused us of trying to sink them.

Save that Aggie suffered severely from mal de mer during the experience, there were no untoward results, and I have simply recounted the affair to explain Charlie Sands' speech.

The fact is that for some time Tish had been growing restless again, and all of us had noticed it. To turn her mind to fishing, then, seemed to offer a safe outlet for those energies which with Tish are prone to translate themselves into action.

For three or four days, therefore, we were very

hopeful. Then, one Thursday afternoon, on her day
out, Hannah came in to see us. She has lived with
Tish so long that she knows her every mood, and
there was a certain wildness in her eye that set
Aggie to sneezing at once.

"She's off again, Miss Lizzie," she said.

"What do you mean, Hannah?"

"She's getting ready for something. She bought
a fishing pole—one that comes to pieces—and she's
been practicing with it out the apartment window
for days. She's dropped two worms that I know of
into Mrs. Perkins's charlotte russe that she'd set on
the windowsill below and she's flung an onion into
the Robinson's baby buggy down in the courtyard,
when the baby was in it."

"An onion?" I said faintly.

"Yes'm. That's in Mr. Charlie's book on fishing.
I read it last night after she was in bed. It says you
can catch fish on all sorts of things. It's the way you
throw them in the water that matters. The man that
wrote it's caught 'em on onions and radishes and
ears of corn."

"He's lying," Aggie said sternly. "Even if I saw
a fish eating an ear of corn I wouldn't believe him."

"Liver too," said Hannah in a hollow voice. "She
put some liver on the hook yesterday morning and
the janitor's cat got it. They had to get a veterinary."

We comforted the poor soul as best we might, but
when she had gone Aggie had a nervous chill. She
was certain that something was going to happen
and that we would find ourselves in trouble again.

"She has been doing so well, Lizzie," she said. "Only the other day Mr. Ostermaier spoke about her Sunday-school class and the things she knits for the Old Ladies' Home."

And with that poor Aggie began to cry. She said she was not frightened; that she was thinking of Mr. Wiggins, and how before he fell off that dreadful roof he had liked to dig a can of worms and cut a pole and go fishing; and no nonsense about radishes and ears of corn and killing people's cats and so on, and her hay fever just coming on.

That was on Thursday. On Friday Tish herself came around. Save that her bonnet was slightly over one ear, she was her usual calm and well-poised self and lost no time in coming to the point.

"For some years," she said, "I have felt that we have not done justice to our great national parks. They are *our* parks. They belong to us, to the people. Year by year thousands of us visit them, gazing on their natural beauties, studying their flora and fauna, and learning something of their great mountains."

Here Aggie, who remembered a trip to Glacier Park some years ago, interrupted her.

"Mountains!" she said bitterly. "Don't you talk mountains to me, Tish Carberry. The next time I propose to drop a set of teeth three thousand feet I'll go up in a balloon and throw them out."

"In proposing the Yellowstone," Tish went on, ignoring her. "I have two reasons. First, there is beauty without danger, and also there is fishing. We are no longer young, and it is as well to prepare for the days to come when the active life may be beyond us. A great mind specialist has said that he never fears for those who like to fish. Aggie, of course, will always belong to those of whom it was said: 'A primrose by a river's brim a yellow primrose was to him, and it was nothing more.'"

"Yellow primrose!" said Aggie furiously. "Yellow goldenrod, you mean. And ragweed, Tish Carberry. And you know perfectly well what they do to me."

"There are also animals," Tish said. "Indeed, I gather that the animals are a great attraction. Kindness has tamed them, and in many cases they will eat out of the human hand."

"Eat a piece out of the human hand!" said Aggie. "What kind of animals?"

"Mostly bears, I believe," Tish told her kindly. "Of course, there are others." But the thought was almost too much for Aggie. She has a great fear of animals, and especially of bears, and into the bargain she has always suffered from hay fever following any visit to the Zoo, maintaining that their fur has a peculiar, irritant quality. Nor was she consoled by the fact that we were to motor across the continent, camping by various streams where Tish might fish and carrying our outfit in a small cart or wagon which trailed behind.

"She'll fish and we'll work," she said most unfairly. "And I'm through with sleeping on the ground. The next time I get into bed with a snake—"

"It was a toad," I reminded her.

"Well, it *felt* like a snake."

Of course, she went in the end, although she was depressed throughout the preparations, buying her knickerbockers, cap, and flannel shirts without enthusiasm and insisting on taking an air mattress. As, however, during revolver practice on the road a few days out, Tish unfortunately put a bullet through it, its usefulness was early over.

But in spite of her apprehension, the trip itself was almost without incident. Some one or two small things occurred, naturally. Thus, Tish always drives her car with sureness but at a high rate of speed, and once we were almost apprehended. Had she not, by a skillful turn of the wheel, forced the motorcycle policeman into a ditch full of water, we would undoubtedly have found ourselves in difficulty. And again, entering a cornfield in search of bait one early morning, she practically collided with the farmer who owned the field.

I must say he was most unpleasant and threatened to have her arrested. But when she explained that she only wanted one ear of corn to fish with he gave her a strange look and backed away.

"Well, all the queer fish aren't in the water," he said. "All right, ma'am, it's yours. But take my advice: I'm a fisherman myself. Put some butter and salt on it, and you want to look for a fish with a good set of teeth."

He waited until Tish had adjusted her hook and dropped it into the hole, and when a moment or two later she drew in a large bass he sat down on the bank and held his head in his hands.

"And me feedin' corn to hogs!" he groaned.
"Man and boy, for fifty years feedin' corn to hogs."

When we broke camp and moved on he was still
there.

We reached the park without incident, and at
once left the main roads for back lanes, where, as
Tish so rightly said, we could be alone with Nature.
Looking back, it is as though we had been led to this
course, for had we not done so we would never have
met Mr. Armstrong, and this account would never
have been written.

Never shall I forget that first meeting. It happened in this fashion:

The roads had grown rougher, and we had been
having trouble with the trailer, which was inclined
to slip and bounce. Indeed, on turning a corner one
day it skidded around and struck a man in a light
buggy. Fortunately he was not injured by his fall,
but after that, on such roads, Tish requested Aggie
to sit on the trailer and thus steady it. It was at such
a time that the meeting occurred.

We were moving along quietly when we saw a
cowboy sitting by the road on his horse. From a
distance he was indeed a gorgeous picture, wearing
orange-colored chaps of some long fur, a purple
shirt, a green neckerchief, and an enormous Stetson
hat. It was only later that we perceived a certain in-
congruity in his costume. At the time all we noticed
was that he held in his hand the loop of a lasso, and
that as we passed he suddenly flung it at the car. A
moment later we heard a terrible cry from Aggie,
and Tish at once put on the brakes. There was our

poor friend, sitting upright in the road with a noose around her neck, and the most shocked expression I have ever seen on a human face.

The cowboy had not moved. He appeared stunned, but after a moment or two he got slowly off his horse and took off his hat.

"Sorry," he said. "Awfully sorry. I didn't know the lady was there."

"You threw that rope at me," Tish said angrily. "Don't stand there and say you didn't. I saw you."

"I was practicing."

"Practicing! Why don't you get a cow to practice on? That's your business, isn't it?"

"Not by a damn sight," he said, with sudden violence. "I'm a — but it's a long story, ladies. A long, sad story. Why should I bother you with my troubles? You can get a ranger about half a mile from here and have me locked up. As a matter of fact, I wish you would. A nice quiet cell somewhere sounds all right to me."

Well, when we had a good look at him, he was certainly a queer figure, for all his fancy clothes. He was a pale young man with nose glasses; not bad-looking but, as Tish said later, all wrong. He had the best of his chaps somewhere up around his armpits, and along with the regulation bag of Bull Durham in the breast pocket of his shirt he had a fountain pen clamped to it. His hat was creased wrong and sat up on top of his head, and when he tried to get on his horse again he started from the off side.

"That's wrong," Tish called to him.

"Is it?" he said humbly. "Thanks. Thanks very much. Maybe that's the reason I've had so much trouble with him."

Well, as he got on he scraped the creature's back with his spur—he had the longest spurs I have ever seen—and the last we saw of him he had picked himself up and the horse was a quarter of a mile away and still going.

II

Of the Yellowstone I need not speak. Who has not seen, in magazines and railroad folders, the pictures of its scenc beauties?

We camped near a basin where there were a number of boiling springs, and here we did our washing. It was a fine sight to see the garments boiled and emerging in a state of snowy whiteness. We erected our clothesline in a grove near by, and as the garments were sucked down out of sight, we waited until they emerged and then hooked them out.

I regret to say, however, that a pair of my own undergarments did not reappear. They had been made by hand, and I was deeply regretful. Later, however, they came back. A very nice young ranger was showing the pool to some girls from a boarding school, and threw in a rather soiled handkerchief so that they could see it sucked down and returned to him clean.

We were sitting near by when this happened.

"Now am I telling you a fairy tale?" he demanded. "There it is! Let's see what's happened to it?"

Well, what had happened was plenty, for when he hooked it out it was my lost undergarment. I never saw a man so upset.

Thus a week passed. We moved from lake to stream and vice versa, but we had not seen the cowboy again, although we often spoke of him. Aggie was particularly interested, scenting a romance, but Tish was busy with her fishing. She caught several trout on radishes and even, one day when we ran short, an excellent one on a dill pickle. Pine cones, however, perhaps because of their lack of color, were not successful.

When she came home in the evening we made it a point to have an excellent meal ready, and to have the camp in perfect order. And on just such an evening, as we were sitting down to dinner, we found the cowboy again.

I was taking some hot biscuits out of the oven when we heard a sound, and he emerged into the firelight. He looked even queerer than before, and he was dragging behind him about six feet of vine that had caught in one of his spurs.

Just as he came close he put one foot on the vine and nearly fell.

"Damn!" he said. "Two or three damns and a hell! Why in the name of the great god Pan anybody *chooses* to wear these things—"

"Then why wear them?" Tish said coldly. "As for your language, you owe us an apology, young man."

"I'm sorry," he said. "The truth is, I'm not quite myself. I've been living on canned beans for a week, and if I keep on I'll need to be roped to the ground or I'll blow away with the first gale."

Well, as supper was ready, we asked him to eat with us, and I never saw a man eat like that. He ate sixteen biscuits, and at the end he seemed much stronger. Not that he cheered perceptibly. What Aggie called a blue-and-yellow melancholy was perceptible throughout, and he had a queer habit, too, of looking over his shoulder. Every time he took a biscuit he would glance about and then pop it into his mouth, all at once.

As Tish said later, he looked haunted.

He was quieter when the meal was over. He took out a package of papers and a bag of tobacco and started to roll a cigarette. Then he muttered something, looked around again, and having put the stuff away, reached down into his boot and took out a box of ready-made cigarettes. When he had lighted one he drew a long breath and looked at us.

"You look like sensible women," he said, "and truthful ones. Tell me, do I look like anything you ever saw before? Like a cowboy, for example, or a strong brutal he-man?"

"From a distance—" Tish began tactfully, but he only groaned.

"Precisely," he said. "From a distance. But I don't fool anybody, do I?" He looked down bitterly at himself. "It's no use. I've been going around like this for two weeks, but it doesn't get any better. Take these chaps. I don't need protection in front.

I need it from the rear; but suppose I do the sensible thing and turn them around! Take these spurs. I'm not used to them, ladies. When I try to hold onto my horse with my legs, and God knows it's the only way I can, I dig him in the ribs and he runs off with me." He sighed. "I've been run off with six times today. Great Scott, what's that?"

We had all heard a rustling in the bushes, but it ceased and he looked relieved. Tish was regarding him intently.

"Are we to understand that you are wearing this costume as a disguise?"

He grunted and shifted his position.

"I can't seem to learn to sit on the ground," he said, "and as to sitting on my heel, which I'm supposed to do, how can any human being sit on a six-inch spur? No, not a disguise, exactly. The truth is—"

But he did not finish. A black bear at that moment came out of the bushes and went toward him. He fairly turned white.

"I'm sorry, ladies," he said. "I've been trying to lose this creature for four days. If you have any candy or sugar, it will keep her quiet. I've given her all I have."

Aggie had screamed and now started to sneeze, but Tish with her usual efficiency at once found some lump sugar. While the bear ate it the young man regarded her with hostile eyes.

"It's a queer world," he said. "I've bought that bear, heart and soul, for four pounds of marshmallows and two jars of honey. But people are different, women especially. Four pounds of marshmallows and two jars of honey! A man can offer a girl all he's got, and she'll want something different."

"Then you are not a cowboy by profession?" Tish asked.

"Cowboy! Ladies, I'll be honest. Since I was ten years old the only acquaintance I've had with a beef steer has been on the plate, not the hoof.

"I'm an Easterner," he went on. "In the bond business. High grade-bonds offering good returns. We specialize in chain stores. There is no question but that the chain store is the future development of the retail business. A bond is income plus security. Also— I'm sorry, ladies! It's the habit of years. Well, about a year ago I became engaged, but a month or so ago the engagement was broken. She came west in June, and she wrote me a letter. She said she had been thinking things over, and I was not the type. The type!" He groaned again, and taking off his enormous hat, held his head in his hands. "What she wants, it appears, is a man who *is* a man; somebody from the open spaces. A man who loves the wild, can conquer a horse, and roll his own cigarettes! Somebody who wears fur pants and likes beans, by heck! I'd like to feed *her* on a bean diet for a week! As a matter of fact, she hates beans. Beans and bears. I'd like to give her Susie for four days. She'd be as fed up as I am."

"Susie?"

"Susie's the bear," he said somberly. "I named her Susie. It was all I could think of. You see, *her* name is Suzanne."

He got up then and gave a hitch to his chaps.

"I don't get the hang of the things," he said mournfully. "If I put my spurs on first in the morning, I can't get 'em on at all. I've tried sleeping in them, but when a man's been accustomed all his life to taking off his pants at night—"

Here Aggie sneezed, and he got up.

"Well, I guess I'll be going," he said.

He thanked us for our hospitality and started off. He had a camp near by, he said. At the edge of the clearing, however, he stopped and looked back.

"You wouldn't like to keep Susie for a while, I suppose?" he said. "She's an interesting bear. You wouldn't believe it, but she stole a bottle of whisky from a tourist's car last Tuesday and brought it back for me to open."

Tish stiffened somewhat.

"And you opened it?"

"Of course, I did," he said. "Don't all these he-men drink whisky?"

Tish was thoughtful after he had gone.

"It is a pitiful case," she said. "Here is a young man whose character is being entirely undermined by some idiot of a girl. He drinks, he swears, he is accessory to a theft. Yet in the past, I feel sure, his life has been blameless."

"If only the girl could see him now," Aggie said gently.

But Tish glared at her.

"The only thing we can hope," she stated, "is that she does not see him."

We retired thoughtfully. I could see that Tish was pondering his problem, and at such times we allow her splendid intellect to work uninterrupted. Things were quiet enough until 2 A. M., when I heard Aggie screaming. As I ran toward her tent something large and lumbering crashed into me and knocked me down. Aggie maintained that Susie had come back and sat down on her chest while she devoured a jar of cold cream and that she had carried off a package of Seidlitz powders. Aggie was considerably unnerved, but no damage had been done, and we went to sleep again.

While we were breakfasting the young man came back.

"See here," he said. "I came to warn you. Are you sure your sugar is all right? I think Susie's poisoned. She went down to the creek this morning to take a drink of water, and I've never seen a bear act like that. She's rolling around now, yelling and foaming at the mouth."

We explained about the Seidlitz powders. He was greatly relieved and ate a hearty breakfast of fish balls and hot waffles. But he seemed abstracted, at that.

He said that he had seen a car go by an hour or so ago and was certain Suzanne was in it, alone.

"As certain as a man can be," he said. "In my condition all girls look like her, of course; but she wore a red tam-o'-shanter, and the way she held her head, and her pretty little nose, and all that—and I know the very way she drives a car, as if she was thinking of something else."

"I consider that very hopeful," Tish said. "She has evidently followed you."

But he shook his head.

"She doesn't know I'm here," he said. "What I had planned was to get this stuff by heart and then spring it on her. She's been at a ranch near Cody, and I was going there later. I meant to ride in, rolling a cigarette with one hand and firing a six-shooter with the other—whatever a six-shooter is. You can't buy anything but automatics now. But what's the use? I can't roll a cigarette with both hands, and when I do I can't make them stick. I've got a tube of library paste, but it tastes something awful."

"Have you any idea where she is going?"

"None whatever. She was going to camp, from the look of her car."

"Camp alone?"

"Oh, she'll start alone, all right," he said listlessly, "but it won't be for long. There will be rangers six feet deep around her in time. She's that kind."

Well, he went away, and Tish, who was looking thoughtful, went fishing. The day was quiet, except for one incident. I was stirring up a cup custard for our evening meal when we heard a horse galloping wildly through the woods. Mr. Armstrong was on him—we had learned that this was his name—and just as the horse passed us he fell off. He lay quite still, and we rushed up to him, but he was unhurt. He was simply lying there swearing quietly but terribly. I was glad that our dear Tish was not present. When he sat up he announced that he was through.

"I've stood a lot," he said. "I've been stung by wasps and thrown from horses and lived on beans and got a bear I don't know what to do with. Enough's enough."

As he was in no condition even to heat a can of beans, we prevailed upon him to take supper with us; Tish brought in a nice string of fish, and Aggie made a sauce tartare. I thought he would never stop eating, and as Susie had not appeared, we had a quiet evening. When he took off his chaps and so on he was a very good-looking young man. He said Suzanne was all right, but that she had been carried away by reading stories about cowboys on dude ranches, and so on.

"It's in her blood now," he said gloomily. "I wrote her that the bond business was fair, and she wrote back that nobody could think of bonds who had sat on a horse and looked at the stars! But you can bet your sweet life she doesn't look at the stars alone."

"She's doing it tonight," Tish reminded him.

"How do you know that?" he demanded. "I'd like to bet she's got three rangers pointing out the Dipper to her this minute. And she'll let on she never saw it before. That's the sort she is."

The next day he was gone. How he escaped from Susie I do not know, but I do know that she remained with us. Aggie never liked her, however, and one day Tish and I, having been to a near-by settlement for food, returned to find our poor Aggie hanging from the branch of a tree, while Susie stood on it and playfully swayed it up and down.

However, she was really a good-natured bear, and she was very useful to us later on.

III

It must have been ten days later that we happened on Suzanne. We had been moving about with Susie on the trailer, camping here and there, and we found her quite by accident.

We had drawn into a grove beside a lake to make camp when we heard a ukelele at a short distance, and a girl singing. Tish motioned us to be quiet, and when we had made our way through the trees we came in sight of her. She was not alone, and just as we got within earshot a male voice said:

"It's a great place to see the stars. Look, there's the Dipper."

We knew then that it was Suzanne, and she certainly was not alone. There was one ranger setting up her tent and another one washing her dishes. She herself looked very pretty and fresh, sitting on a robe from her car.

"There's one thing I'll say for you western men," she said. "You can do everything, from washing dishes to firing a gun. When I think of the men I know back home, sitting around clubs or playing golf, it makes me sick."

"It's sure the life, little girl."

She sighed and looked pensive.

"When I think that I have to go back to *that*," she said. "I who adore the open and the stars! Picture me at balls this next winter! I who so love the wild, and the creatures of the wild. The big shaggy buffaloes, the gentle deer, the cunning friendly bears."

Just at that instant Susie walked into the clearing toward her, and she let out the most awful yell.

"It's a bear!" she screamed. "It's coming at me! Shoot it, somebody."

As we retired from the spot Tish's indignation was extreme.

"The little fool," she said furiously. "What a man like Mr. Armstrong can see in a girl like that is beyond me. She needs a lesson, that's what she needs. Camping! I'll bet somebody else has cooked every slice of bacon for her since she got here. What she needs—"

She did not complete the sentence, but remained in deep thought during the remainder of the evening.

The next day was a repetition of that evening. The rangers being presumably occupied, two young men in plus fours did Suzanne's camp work and listened to her ukulele, and in the evening three rangers came. As she was a very pretty girl, probably this was to be expected, but Tish resented it with what in anyone less broad of mind would have been sulkiness. She did not fish that day, but remained in camp, and late that night I wakened to see Susie tied to a tree, an unusual procedure, and Tish poring by the firelight over what appeared to be a map.

As I was weary I slept heavily and was only roused by Aggie bending over me and shaking me.

"She's gode!" she said, excitement always causing her an acute coryza. "Tish's gode and she's left a dote. Oh, Lizzie, there's sobethig wrog. Sobethig terribly wrog."

The note told us very little. Tish had found it expedient to go to the cabin—an isolated spot in a remote corner of the park where we had once spent two days—and would meet us there later in the day at the crossroads. "Bring Susie," she wrote. "Also some canned beans and half a dozen packages of marshmallows. But do not come to the cabin. *Stop at the crossroads.*"

"Stop at the crossroads!" Aggie said indignantly. "I'be stoppig right here. If she thigks I'be goig to walk fifty biles draggig that bear by the had she can thigk agaid."

It was not necessary to walk, however, as we found that Tish *had not taken the car.* Our bewilderment was extreme, but there was nothing to do but obey. I can drive a little, and so we proceeded to break camp and prepare to depart. Here a most untoward incident occurred, probably due to my preoccupation. In attempting to start I unluckily put the car into reverse, and to my horror we backed rapidly down a bank and into the lake.

In this connection I should like to say that, Aggie notwithstanding, we were never in any danger whatever. By standing upright in the car our heads were well above the surface, and Susie indeed appeared to enjoy it. I recall that in some manner or other she caught a fish and ate it with apparent gusto.

Nevertheless, time was lost. It was fully two hours before a passing car discovered us and pulled us out. And while waiting we had abundance of time in which to discuss the mystery. Aggie was convinced that Tish had been abducted and had written the note under duress.

"We bay dever see her agaid," she said dismally.

But I was filled with dire forebodings which I kept to myself. From where we stood in the water we could see Suzanne's camp site, and it appeared to be deserted. Also there was no sign of her car, and once more in agony of mind I saw our dear Tish as I had seen her the night before, poring over a map.

It was late in the evening and raining when we reached the crossroads, but there to our joy was our comrade, safe and sound. True, she looked worn and somewhat battered, as though she had been through a struggle of some sort, and there was a long scratch across her cheek. But she was cheerful, and almost exalted.

"Did you bring the beans and marshmallows?" was her first question.

She listened absently to our explanation of our delay, glanced at Susie asleep in the rear of the car, and at once took the wheel.

"We shall have to take a roundabout route," she

said. "I came by a short cut on foot, but with the car— You haven't seen Mr. Armstrong, I suppose?"

"No," I said.

"Well, that can wait."

It was then raining hard, and the road was growing worse. We rattled over rocks and sank into mudholes, and once Aggie wailed that Susie was holding onto her and squeezing her to death. But it was not until dusk had fallen that we finally mired in a deep hole, and nothing Tish could do was of any avail. We were in a remote portion of the park, far from any tourist travel, and to add to our discomfort a cold wind was blowing.

It was quite dark when Tish finally abandoned the effort and walked ahead to look for a camping spot. When she returned there was hope in her voice.

"There's a cow lying in the road just around the bend," she said. "If I can slip a rope over its horns it will pull us out. A cow is tractable, but strong."

I immediately got out the towrope, and Tish made a loop in it. Then we tied the free end to the car, and she disappeared into the darkness. It was only an instant later that things began to happen. There was a terrible jerk, and Susie was hurtled into the air and out into the road. The next moment I saw Tish running toward us.

"Untie that rope!" she called. "It's not a cow. It's a—"

I heard no more. We were off on the wildest ride in my experience. For some little time the creature kept to the road. Then it turned, and of what followed I have only a dim and confused memory. Once I am sure we went through a stream, and again over a burned forest. It is well enough for Tish to ask why I did not set the brakes; so far as I recall I was not stationary in one spot long enough to set anything. I do not even know when I lost Aggie.

But all is well that ends well. At the end of two miles, according to Tish's later estimate, the car brought up against a tree and the rope broke. I could hear the creature galloping off, and knew that the adventure was over. Nevertheless, it was some time before I could compose myself, and almost dawn before I was able to sleep. The day had been an eventful one, and I am not as young as I once was.

At daybreak Tish and Aggie found me, having had no difficulty in tracing my progress. Tish said that the rope was over the creature's horns before she realized that it was a large buffalo, probably male, and that it was then too late to do anything.

She examined the car, and found that, except for losing its lamps and mudguards, it was still intact.

"They are certainly powerful animals," she said thoughtfully. "And how the Indians ever killed them with bows and arrows I cannot understand. However—"

She then inspected our location, and declared that if we had chosen it it could not have been better. With which cryptic remark we set to work to make camp, asking no questions. Tish herself had disappeared, taking with her the beans and marsh-mallows. When she returned we were astounded to find that she had brought with her a number of camp delicacies in cans and bottles, but she offered no explanations.

Indeed, almost her sole remark, I recall, during the evening was when she asked if we had any idea of where Mr. Armstrong was to be located. When we said we had not, she frowned slightly.

"He must be found," she said. "Not necessarily at once, but soon. If only the idiot hasn't left the park! It would be like a man," she continued, with that clear vision of the other sex which never fails her, "to let somebody else do the work and take the risks, and then run off."

It was the next morning that Aggie, whose day it was to police the camp, came to me with an ago-nized look on her face. Tish was again absent on one of her mysterious errands.

"She was out last night, Lizzie," she said. "I saw her go. And she took Susie with her, on a rope."

"If you *will* spy on her," I began, but she inter-rupted me by holding out a piece of cloth with two small holes cut in it.

"Do you know what that is?" she demanded. "It's a mask, and Tish had it on last night. Where did she go? Where did she get six cans of caviar, three bottles of olives, and all that deviled ham? She didn't win it in a raffle."

And just then Tish came into camp and heard her. If she was indignant she concealed it, and her voice was kindly, even tolerant, when she spoke.

"The question is an ethical one, Aggie," she said, "and probably beyond your comprehension. But it is this: when I find a problem with a possible honorable and happy solution I feel that I am satisfied in going to any lengths to work it out."

"What lengths?" Aggie demanded in a terrible voice.

"I have removed Suzanne from an environment obviously unsuited to her, and certainly unsettling. She is safe at the cabin; she has a roof over her head, beans to eat and coffee to drink, and a bunk to sleep in. If she knows enough to fill it with leaves she will have a good bed. All she lacks is men to do the work for her and show her the Dipper."

"And you think she'll stay?" Aggie asked scornfully. "She's got a car, hasn't she?"

I shall never forget the forbearance in Tish's voice as she replied.

"She has indeed a car, Aggie. Unfortunately, it has no gasoline in it."

"She's got two legs. If everybody doesn't know that, it's not *her* fault."

"But Susie has four," said Tish kindly. "It is strange how she dislikes Susie, for Susie likes the cabin. All I have done has been to throw a few marshmallows on the roof at night, and it is really surprising how much time that bear spends on it."

Well, it appeared that she considered Suzanne really a nice girl, only temporarily gone wrong, and that she felt that a brief lesson, with Mr. Armstrong later effecting a rescue, was the only thing needed.

Later on, she told us further details. Of the kidnaping she said little, save that it had been necessary only to threaten Suzanne with a revolver, and that the girl had showed considerable courage. She had indeed thought that Tish was a man and had tried a number of small coquetries on her, but naturally without effect.

But Tish felt that Mr. Armstrong ought to play a part in all this and that the first thing, naturally, was to find him. Her plan was to leave Aggie and myself on guard, so to speak, and herself take the car and locate him if possible. She had found a vantage spot on the hill over the cabin, and there we were to watch, unseen. To prevent a chance intruder from driving into the cabin lane, she had already set up a sign, "Keep out. Danger." And she felt that all was well.

Early the next morning, therefore, she took her departure, and Aggie and I began our vigil. Only a day or so ago I found my notes, as I had kept them.

"Monday, Aug. 3rd: S. waited inside the cabin until Susie got off the roof and departed. Then she gathered firewood, but it was green and would not burn. Cried a bit. Made fire at last. Put coffee on and opened can of beans. Coffeepot upset and coffee spilled. Got more water for coffee from creek. Beans burned while doing so. Gave up, kicked coffeepot and upset it. Has had nothing so far all day. On Susie appearing again, ran into cabin.

"Tuesday: Tried to wash some clothes in creek. Lost soap, as it floated away. Followed it for a time, then gave up in despair. Imagine it is only soap she has. Large moose around cabin today. Wonder if Tish thought of this possibility? She has given up trying to build fire and is eating cold beans out of tin cans. Evidently loathes them, but needs nourishment.

"Wednesday: She has been trying to gather firewood for cabin, as nights are cold. Dropped a piece on her foot and sat down and cried. More beans. In intervals between Susie has been carrying leaves into cabin. Looks pretty dreadful. Hair all out of curl and face black with smoke. Stopped gathering leaves today to shake her fist at mountains.

"Later: In desperation, at 3 P. M. made attempt to escape. Filled pockets with cans of beans, looking at them with hatred, and got hat and coat. I was obliged to rouse Susie from sleep and send her down. Think she is out of cigarettes, as Aggie saw her powdering dried leaves and rolling them in paper."

IV

When we got back that evening Tish was in camp. She stated that Mr. Armstrong was on the way, and that he had wanted to come in the car, but she had persuaded him otherwise.

"If he is to rescue her," she said, "it should be done gallantly. And this is his one chance to assert his superiority. He should dash in and, more or less, throw her over his saddle and gallop away."

I regret to say that here Aggie laughed. Tish looked at her coldly.

"You think it funny?" she inquired. "With two young lives to make or break, you can laugh?"

Aggie sobered at once, and we made our reports. Tish seemed satisfied, and in the glow of her approval we sat about preparing the evening meal. It was after we had eaten that an incident occurred which had an important bearing on the next event. Susie had come in and was looking for scraps, and as she got in the way Aggie struck her sharply on the nose. *But it was not Susie.* It reared up to an enormous height, and we then saw that it was a silvertip, or grizzly, the most dangerous of all bears.

However, our dear Tish is always reliable in an emergency. While it was still standing, waving its paws and growling, she hurriedly took the top off the pepperbox and flung several handfuls of pepper toward it. It at once began to sneeze and soon beat a retreat, but our poor Aggie also inhaled some and was in great distress for several hours.

It was late that night when Mr. Armstrong got in, and I don't know when I've seen a man look so unhappy. The way he glared at his horse when he had crawled off it was simply poisonous.

"Aren't you going to unsaddle him?" Tish asked.

"No," he said bitterly. "Let him sleep in his clothes. I do."

"Sit down and you'll feel better."

"Sit?" he said. "Sit! I don't wish to be indelicate, ladies, but to the best of my knowledge and belief my sitting days are over." He then looked about him, and sighed. "But if you have a nice hollow somewhere handy for my right hipbone, I'll lie down."

Well, he looked terrible. I don't know when he had shaved, and the orange fur of his chaps was simply filled with burrs. Also, he said that he felt itchy all over and that he was liable to poison ivy.

"But it may only be hives again," he observed gloomily. "I've had them off and on, or rather in and out, for a week."

He was more cheerful after we'd made him some coffee. He said that if he had the luck to get home with his sanity intact the only horse he would ride hereafter would plug into a lamp socket, and at last he asked about Suzanne. He listened intently while we told him.

"And no rangers?" he asked wonderingly. "No ukulele and no Dipper? Are you sure you got the right girl?"

When we reassured him he drew a long breath. "Ladies," he said, "you have worked a miracle. And beans? You said beans? She hates 'em. She always did. And they're starchy too. She doesn't eat starches."

And then at last he lay back and laughed, for the first time since we had known him. He was quite nice when he laughed. He had good teeth and he really looked very boyish.

"Now let me get this," he said. "All I have to do is to ride in, throw her over the pommel of the saddle—or the cantle, I never can remember which it is—and carry her off. Is that it?"

"You'll have to carry her off *from* something," Tish observed.

"You bet your sweet life I will," he said heartily. "From rangers and cowboys and all the male sons of guns who have turned her pretty little head out here."

"You'll have to rescue her."

"Rescue's my middle name." He lay still and looked up at the sky. "You see," he said, "she's all right, back home. She's more than that; she's wonderful. And I had her, all right. No Dipper business either. I never could find the damned thing in the sky. It's only this summer—"

His voice trailed off, and Aggie, who always loves a lover, put a blanket over him as he slept.

While I worked over his chaps that night, combing them and removing the dead leaves, small twigs, burrs, and certain insects which he had picked up, Tish at last told us of her plan. On the following night, from the hillside, we were to fire a number of shots, being careful to shoot into the air. Then, in the midst of what must appear to be a deadly attack, Mr. Armstrong was to ride to the rescue.

"He ought to be able to do that," she said. "Even a man in the bond business should be able to ride a hundred yards. But he must shave and have a haircut. I can cut his hair; I used to do Charlie Sands' when he was small."

Naturally, she emphasized the need of haste. Nobody could tell when some ranger would ride in, or a tourist disregard the sign and discover Suzanne. We retired at last, although I have reason to believe that Tish made a final excursion that night, scattering marshmallows around the cabin as well as on the roof, and that to this may be laid certain of our later difficulties.

Unfortunately, when Mr. Armstrong wakened the next morning it was evident that the attack would have to be delayed. Poison ivy or hives, both his eyes were swollen almost shut; after retiring into the woods, he returned to say that his entire body was in a similar condition. He had even lost interest in Suzanne, and as he felt better in water, he spent a part of the day immersed in the creek.

Tish carried his lunch there, and placed it on a boulder at a distance. She said he was quite pathetic, and that even if Suzanne wandered so far—which was unlikely—she would never recognize him. Also, that he was almost frozen as the water came from a glacier above.

The delay was trying, but by the next day, Aggie having made him starch poultices for the worst spots, he was much better.

We made a reconnaissance that day, and my notes are as follows:

"Friday: She has apparently taken a dislike to the cabin, and has spent most of the day in her car, with doors and windows closed. So far as observable has eaten nothing all day, nor built a fire. Through glasses her expression is desperate. Advise immediate action."

As a result, the attack was set for that night, and we spent the remainder of the day in grooming Mr. Armstrong. Fortunately, Tish found a pair of clip-

pers in her odds-and-ends box and was able to give
him an excellent western haircut, running the clip-
pers well up the back of his head and over his ears
and leaving a heavy thatch above. This so changed
his appearance that when she gave him the mirror
he almost dropped it.

He did not seem very pleased, observing that his
hair grew slowly and that it was all right to be
thorough, but not too damned thorough. And when
he found that his hat was now slightly too large
for him he seemed even more upset.

"Well," he said, "thank God I've got ears. If I
hadn't I'd have to wear it around my neck and
cut eyeholes in the crown. However——"

By nightfall everything was ready, and we moved
in single file to the brow of the hill. All was still
below, and a young moon bathed the landscape in
faint beauty. But all was not well with us. As we
approached the edge Mr. Armstrong's horse gave
undeniable signs of being nervous, and Mr. Armstrong himself was undoubtedly uneasy.

"See here," he said, "why can't I simply run
down after the shooting and save her? What do I
need a horse for? I've about as much chance of
carrying her off on the cantle——"

"Pommel," Tish corrected him.

"On the pommel, as I have of growing an extra
pair of legs. Not that I couldn't use 'em if I had
them. It would take a fellow with four legs to sit
this beast."

But Tish was insistent, and he was finally able
to mount. None of us, I fear, had the faintest idea

of what was to come, but we had no more than fired
the first volley when the horse bolted at a terrific
rate. Luckily, if there can be any luck in such a
situation, it headed directly down the hillside and
toward the cabin, and Tish directed us to hold our
fire and to listen. So far as we could tell, however,
it did not pause at the cabin, or even hesitate, and
we were left to face a dire and ignominious failure.

It was not until we had waited for some hours,
and neither Mr. Armstrong nor the horse had returned, that our brave Tish decided to make an in-
vestigation, creeping down the hillside, she disappeared from our sight.

We did not see her again for many hours!

Never shall I forget those hours of tension. Dawn
found us still there, and revealed no sign of life
below. Our dear Tish, Mr. Armstrong, and his
horse had vanished, and our hearts were fairly sick
with apprehension.

Nor was this lessened when Aggie suddenly
caught me by the arm and, sneezing violently,
pointed beneath.

Suzanne was getting out of the car and slowly
and warily approaching the cabin. When almost
there, we saw her stop and pick up something;
catching up the field glasses, we saw that it was a
revolver. Undoubtedly the one we had lent Mr.
Armstrong, and which must have been shaken from
its holster during his wild ride.

But what was our horror to see her level the gun
at the cabin door, and pull the trigger, not once but
twice. Had she heard movement within, and was

Tish, that dauntless woman, inside the cabin and at her mercy? We could not tell.

I draw a curtain over the following three hours. Suzanne had once more retired to her car, but never relaxed her vigilance. However, from where she sat the roof of the cabin was hidden from her, and it was here that we at last perceived signs of life. A shingle or two were seen to move, and through this came a dear familiar hand, waving cautiously to us. She lived. Our beloved Tish lived and awaited rescue.

"We must save her, Aggie," I said. "We must get that girl away."

"I'm not going near her," Aggie retorted. "She's dangerous. Anyhow, that's Mr. Armstrong's job, although what he wants of a hellcat like that is beyond me."

"She'd be gentle enough if she had some real food, Aggie."

"She can starve to death for all of me," Aggie retorted bitterly.

But what else was there to do? I finally proposed that we wander in on her from the rear, pretending to be picking flowers, and that we then attempt to coax her with us to camp, holding out the inducement of a hot meal. This we proceeded to do. We had one bad moment, however, for we were close behind her when Aggie, who is susceptible to certain of the wild flowers, sneezed violently. Suzanne whirled and fired at us point-blank, and the bullet knocked my flowers out of my hand. But the next moment she had dropped the revolver, and such a

look of relief was observable in her face that my
heart was touched.

"Sorry!" she said. "Apologies and so on. I didn't
sleep last night and I'm a trifle nervy."

"Dervy!" said Aggie, sneezing again. "If that's
all you cad say, after tryig to shoot two idoffedsive
wobed—"

"This is no place for inoffensive women," she
said briskly. "With game poachers shooting all
around and a grizzly bear in my cabin."

Aggie opened her mouth to speak, but I silenced
her.

"A bear? Are you sure it is a bear?" I asked
gently.

"Of course, it's a bear," she said, eying me.
"This place is full of bears. I didn't know there
were so many bears in the world. When I get out
of here I'm heading back east, and the only reason
I'm not flying there this minute is because I haven't
got wings. By the way," she added, trying to look
casual, "I'm offering a premium on ham and eggs
and twenty gallons of gas, if you know of either in
these parts."

When I said we had both, she almost burst into
tears. She didn't look or act like the girl with the
ukulele, and later on we found the thing; it looked
as though she had deliberately put her foot through
it. She went with us without a question; indeed, she
said very little on the way to camp, except once
when Aggie mentioned rangers.

"Rangers!" she said. "Don't talk to me about
rangers. I've been kidnaped, starved, and lost for a

week, and has any ranger taken the trouble to look
me up? He has not."

Well, she was half famished, and after she had
eaten, and borrowed some soap and taken a bath,
she looked like a different girl. But she stuck to her
story about a grizzly bear in her cabin, and both
Aggie and I began to grow uneasy. We knew it
was not Susie, as Susie had been carefully tied up
in the woods and was still there, and at last Aggie
slipped away and came back with a white face.

"It's true!" she gasped. "And they're both there
with it, Tish and Mr. Armstrong. They're in the
upper bunk. Oh, Lizzie, Lizzie, to think of her at
the mercy of that savage beast!"

"Nonsense! What did she say?"

Suzanne was asleep by that time, and Aggie cautiously felt in her pocket.

"I got on the roof," she said, "and she gave me
this list. She says not to give the girl any coffee
tonight so that she will sleep, and we're to bring
her these things. She hasn't given up, Lizzie. She
said she means to turn defeat into victory. She
made the list with Mr. Armstrong's fountain pen."

"Yes," I said scornfully. "He'd lose his revolver,
but he'd keep his fountain pen. That's men for
you!"

But I confess that the list puzzled me. It, too, lies
before me on my desk, written on the back of an
old envelope. It runs as follows:

(a) Ropes from trailer.
(b) Provisions: flour, baking powder, salt, coffee, condensed milk, bacon, eggs.

(c) Hammer and nails.
(d) Sewing basket.
(e) Reflector oven.
(f) Bottle of glue. (Mr. A's library paste lost from pockets when horse ran away.)
(g) Bottle of cordial.
(h) Large skinning knife.
(i) Revolver.
(j) Bottle of chloroform liniment. (This last being used on occasion by Aggie for her rheumatism.)
(k) Bath sponge.

As Suzanne roused just then, I put the list away, and we prepared supper. It was evident that Tish, while uncomfortable, was in no immediate danger, and so Aggie baked some of her delicious cup custards, and once more Suzanne ate heartily.

But we gave her no coffee, and soon she was yawning again.

"Sorry," she said. "If I ever get back to a decent bed, believe me I'll stay there." She was thoughtful for a moment. "Queer thing, life," she said. "I turned down a—well, a boy friend in the East after I came out here. But he doesn't look so bad to me now. Maybe golf and bonds— They're not exciting, but they're safe."

Here she yawned once more and before long was asleep.

We lost no time in preparing to depart, and soon we were on our way. We were hardly out of camp, however, before Aggie tripped over something and dropped the tin oven, and Suzanne sat up and yelled. I went back and quieted her, and so at last we reached the cabin.

Tish heard us and called to bring the chloroform liniment, sponge, and ropes to the roof. This we did. There followed, in a very short time, a terrific commotion within; indeed, from the voices, it was at one time apparent that the positions had been reversed; that the bear was in the upper bunk and our friends below. But following that came a period of quiet, and the soothing odor of chloroform was noticeable.

It was not long afterward that Tish's buoyant voice called us in, and we were able to light a portion of candle left uneaten by the bear and survey the scene.

The bear, roped and tied, was lying on the floor, and a sponge soaked in liniment was fastened to his nose. The remainder of the cabin was completely wrecked, and standing with his back to a corner was Mr. Armstrong.

"Ladies," he said, "someone has said that the farther he went west the more convinced he felt that the wise men came from the East. In the vernacular, he said a mouthful. I'm through. I'm done. Henceforth I am for the great open spaces of civilization."

But Tish looked at him coldly.

"On the contrary," she said, "you love the West. It cannot be too western for you. You hate selling bonds. You are never going back. You are henceforth a free and untrammeled spirit."

"Oh, have it your own way," he agreed, without

enthusiasm, "But it's going pretty strong to tell any man he's a free and untrammeled spirit when he's had the seat clawed out of his breeches."

"Your breeches will be repaired as soon as you give them to us."

"Ladies!" he said in a shocked voice. "Even a free and un—"

"You can go outside and hand them in."

"Outside?" he said. "In that wind? I don't want to seem to complain, but I'm liable to colds, and as all I have underneath is a pair of unmentionables and one or two adhesive plaster dressings—"

Well, he went finally, but not before he had asked all about Suzanne.

"So she's all right," he said, when we had told him. "And she hates the West, does she? Well, that makes two of us, bless her little heart. And if that's the case, Miss Tish, why any more?"

But Tish was firm. She said that Suzanne was only convalescent, not cured, and that the only thing now was to go on to the bitter end. He agreed finally, and having handed in his garments for repair, proceeded to the roof. As he hammered he insisted that what we heard was his teeth chattering, but Tish ignored this and together we put the cabin in order.

I must confess that we were still in the dark as to what she intended, and it was with some bewilderment that we observed certain of her actions. For example, it will be recalled that, although she never smokes and indeed considers it degrading in a woman, she had learned some years ago to roll a cigarette in western fashion. This she now proceeded to do, rolling a dozen or so and carefully fastening them with glue. At the same time she instructed me to mix up and cut out a batch of biscuits, and to place them in the reflector oven, ready for baking, and when Mr. Armstrong returned she gave him a careful lesson in how to slice bacon and properly break eggs into a frying pan, and also in making coffee.

"If I go on I'll be a good wife for somebody someday," he said.

But he seemed quite cheerful, once indeed standing with his arms folded and his foot on the prostrate bear and asking to have his picture taken.

It was daylight when we left him, and when Suzanne wakened we were getting breakfast. Well, the sleep and a little soap had done wonders for her, and she looked quite pretty again. She eyed Tish, but without suspicion.

"I didn't see you yesterday, did I?" she said.

"No," Tish told her. "I was not here. I was studying the wild life of the West."

Suzanne only yawned and stretched.

"You can have it," she said.

It was after breakfast that Tish told her she had been over to look at the cabin, and there was certainly no bear there. Only a good-looking young man who was building a fire.

"Quite handsome," she said, "and evidently a Westerner from the way he went about things."

Well, Suzanne had brightened at the start, but at the word Westerner her face fell.

"You can have him too," she said morosely.

But later on she stuck her hands in her breeches pockets and started off, and as soon as we were certain she was going to the cabin we followed her at a safe distance. Tish went and got Susie, and took her along on a rope, for some reason of her own, and we were able to get fairly close.

I must say that Mr. Armstrong did us credit. Tish had fixed him before we left, and his chaps were where they ought to be and he had taken off his nose glasses. He had a revolver hanging on his hip and one of the cigarettes Tish had made in his mouth; he had built a fire in front of the cabin and was turning over frying bacon with the skinning knife, which is about a foot long.

Maybe he really did not see her at first without his glasses, for he gave a fine start and said:

"You!"

Well, I don't know that I've ever seen a mortal being look as astonished as she did when she recognized him.

"Jim," she exclaimed. "What in the world—"

"Just a moment," he said. "I don't want these biscuits to burn. Well, this is a surprise! Who'd have expected to see you in this part of the world!"

"You *knew* I was out here."

"That's so too, when I think about it," he said. "Look at those biscuits, little girl. Ever see better biscuits? Yes, I knew you were in the West, but the West's a big place. When I think how much of it I have yet to see— I want to put some eggshells in the coffee."

She stared at him as if she couldn't believe her eyes.

"When did you get here? To this cabin?"

"I dropped in—let's see! It was some time yesterday, wasn't it? Or the day before. I don't pay much attention to time when I'm out like this."

"Was there a bear here when you came?"

"Sure was. Would you like a cup of coffee? I think coffee's at its best in the open, don't you?"

"If you'd only quit babbling," she said angrily. "What became of the bear?"

"He's inside. Roped up. Can't kill a park bear, you know."

Suddenly she sat down on the trunk of a tree and ran her hand over her eyes.

"I think if I had a cigarette—" she said weakly.

"Surest thing you know. Wait a minute and I'll roll one for you. That's what you like, I believe."

He went into the cabin, and coming back presented her with one. He stood watching while she took a puff or two.

"When I think of the Turkish and Egyptian cigarettes I used to smoke," he began, "I— What's the matter with it?"

"It's simply poisonous," she said weakly. "It— it tastes like glue."

He looked offended at that and asked her if she would have some breakfast, but she only shook her head.

"You're sure? No bacon and eggs?"

"Nothing, thanks."

"Well, you don't mind if I eat, do you? One thing I've found out. This open-air life does give one an appetite."

"Does it?" she said without any spirit whatever. "I'm glad you like it. I never thought you would."

"Like it? It's the only life, my dear."

He had poured himself some coffee, and now he sat down on his heel. Unluckily he had forgotten his spurs, and he jumped and dropped his cup. But our dear Tish fortunately created a diversion at the moment. She loosed Susie, and Susie went toward them on the run.

Suzanne leaped and shrieked, but Mr. Armstrong only smiled.

"What!" he said playfully. "Afraid of a common, everyday black bear! Now a grizzly, that's different, but this sort—!"

Here he hit Susie a smart smack on the nose and I thought the girl's eyes would pop out of her head.

"Go away and be a good bear," he said. "Don't you see we have distinguished company? Go in and look at big brother inside, all nicely roped up and everything."

Suzanne was gazing at him fixedly.

"It *is* you, I suppose?" she said. "It looks like you. It sounds like you. But if it *is* you—"

"Why, of course it is, my dear child. If there is any difference, it is that you only knew the office slave, not the man. Thank God, *that's* over."

"The office slave would at least have asked how I got here."

"But, my dear," he said in a hurt voice, "what

business is that of mine? Once, I grant you, I had the right, but now——! You see, Suzanne dear, the East without you was empty, so I came west. Here I have found myself, and here I shall probably stay. I find that I love the wild and the creatures of the wild —just a moment: I'll give the little bear a biscuit— and I dote on the open spaces. Give me a horse and some cans of beans, and I ask no more. Let me sleep under the stars, gazing up at the Dipper and—and the rest of them, and I am happy and content."

"And that's all?"

"That's all, lacking you, my dear."

"And if you had me?"

"I love you, of course," he said. "Perhaps I never really found you until I lost you, if you know what I mean. Alone under the—the Dipper, I can think of you. On my stanch and sturdy horse, following the white trail over the hills, you have belonged to me as never before. I shall always remember you, my dear."

"You'd rather dream of me than have me, I dare say," she said sharply.

"A dream is better than nothing, my darling."

And then she began to cry.

"I can't do it," she wailed. "I love you. I was just a fool, that's all. But I can't stay out here. I want to go home. I want to sleep in a bed and sit in a chair. I want a decent haircut and a manicure, and if I ever see another bean I'll scream. You can take your choice. Me or—or the Dipper."

"And that's final?"

"That's final."

He drew a long breath. Then he started toward her. His spurs caught in a twig and almost threw him, but when he recovered his balance his arms were around her. I looked at our dear Tish, and she was faintly smiling.